La'Mea

"Oh my God!" I yelled with blood covering my hands. What the hell just happened? Why did he charge at me like that? I looked down at the blood spreading on the floor. It was everywhere. I should've never came! How was I going to explain this shit? Carter was going to kill me. So many thoughts were running through my mind. I ran over to my coat and searched for my phone. Fumbling through my messages, I called Jakirra who was waiting outside in the car.

"Damn, I hope you're not fucking that nigga?" Jakirra chuckled as she answered the phone.

"I think he's dead!" I cried out. "Please come in here. Best, I think I killed him."

Jakirra never responded. Moments later, her and DeAsia was standing in the doorway in disbelief. I could tell by the look on their faces they had no idea what the fuck to do.

"La'Mea, what the hell happened?" Jakirra yelled.

"What have you done?" DeAsia asked, getting closer to the body to see if he was really dead. "Did you at least check and see if he had a chance of living? I mean is he really dead?"

They both looked at me awaiting an answer. I still said nothing. I looked over at the body and looked down on the floor. I stood there in silence. All this felt like a bad dream. I never meant for none of this to happen. All I wanted to do was protect the people I loved. This wasn't supposed to happen.

"DeAsia, check and make sure he's dead!" Jakirra ordered.

DeAsia eyes got big as hell. She looked twice at the body then back at Jakirra. She heard what Jakirra asked her to do. She didn't move at first; she looked at both of us and shook her head.

"Umm, bitch, I didn't kill him. I'm definitely ain't about to touch him. Lil crazy better get over here and check and see if he's dead," she rolled her eyes and backed up. "Ya'll got me fucked up. I'm not going to jail with ya'll hoes today. I'm not!"

Jakirra completely tuned her out. She walked over and leaned to examine his body. She looked over at me again.

"Best, I think he's really dead!" she said calmly. "LA'MEA!"

She kept yelling my name. In my head, I wanted to tell her what happened, but I was numb; I didn't move, and I didn't speak. I just stood there in complete silence.

Two Weeks Earlier.....

"Aye girl, you act like you don't fuck with a nigga," Ant said, standing behind me in Walmart.

I shook my head and rolled my eyes. I knew it was just a matter of time before we crossed paths. I was really outdone with his remarks at Carter's party. I wasn't trying to see his ass for real. He was out of line that night.

"Good to see you too," I replied. "How have you been?"

"Nah, don't act like we cool now. Yo ass been playin' the fuck outta crazy. You shoulda been the first person I seen, considering I was fucking you before I got locked up," Ant said, blowing down. "Now your ass is brand new and shit."

I looked at his ass. I mean he was right; he was fucking me before he went to jail, but shit I wasn't the only one. I rolled my eyes at him. He was funny to me. I couldn't believe that I was entertaining his bullshit. He was acting like I was his main bitch or something.

"Oh, boy! I'm sure you had enough hoes to see you when you got out. Please don't go there. Shit, I wasn't the only person you was fucking with." I was sarcastic as I could be.
"We weren't official, Ant, so don't act like that!"

"You love this nigga Carter I keep hearing so much about? You up and got you another nigga like me, huh?"

"Yeah, I love him, but tell me what does that have to do with you doe? Like you're really worried about the wrong things. First you talkin' about how I was supposed to be the first person you shoulda seen, and now you're talkin' bout me lovin' a nigga! Chill!" I replied defensively. "Who I'm loving ain't none of yo' concern."

"I'm just asking, my nigga. I've been home for a minute, and you act like that don't mean shit to you! I mean a nigga can't even get a lunch date or nothing! I thought we was better den that. A nigga can't even be your friend."

He tried to pull me close. I couldn't help but laugh. A lunch date? This fool couldn't be serious. I was more amused than I was showing. I couldn't help but wonder why the nigga cared when the nigga had a whole bitch last time I checked. The nigga was checking for me too hard. I mean, who didn't know that I loved Carter, but shit he was still all in my business.

"Ant, don't act like you don't know how the game go. I gotta nigga now. When you had me, you didn't want me. I mean at least you didn't act like it. You wanted me and every other hoe on Broadway. Now you missed out. That's your fault." I rolled my eyes.

He had completely blew me. He had his nerve. He thought he was going to go to jail and come home and shit was going to be the same. I had moved on to bigger and better things. I wasn't down to be in a love triangle.

"I'm just sayin,' La'Mea. I mean we can at least be friends. We owe each other at least that much." He reached out for my hand. "You don't wanna be my friend? Or will your nigga have a problem with that? I mean you could at least take my number."

He was trying hard. I wanted to tell him hell no because I knew nothing good would come out the situation, but I reached for his phone and added myself as a contact.

"Ima hit you up later."

I watched him walk away. I wanted to ask him who he was with, but it was so packed and I just wanted to get out of there. Something about that didn't really sit well with me, but if he got out of hand he could definitely meet my blocklist.

***

When I finally made it home, it was quiet. I just knew Carter would've been back home already from kicking it with Ced and Cartier. He said they had a few things to take care of, but I swear it felt like he was gone forever. I plopped down on the couch and decided to call my best to see what she was up to.

"Baby, supa supa head!" DeAsia answered on the first ring. "I was just about to call you, but I figured your mouth was getting put in better use!"

"Man shut up!" I cracked up.

This bitch was always talking shit. I couldn't deal with her funny shit. It was so sad because she knew me so fucking well, and her and the dick jokes didn't bother me much because when it came to Carter I loved sucking his dick. I think I loved it more than he did.

"Nah, seriously man, I wanted to know what was up with Cartier's little sexy ass. I saw him and his brothers today at the spot. You know I want parts."

"Girl, leave Cartier alone. He don't want yo ass!" I rolled my eyes. "This ain't all my friends mess with Carter's brothers!"

"Damn! Don't try to hate. You got Carter, and Jakirra be talking to Ced. Damn how come I can't get Cartier! Its only right he fuck with me!" she snickered.

"Yeah whatever. Cartier ain't yo shit!" I assured her. "Anyway, what's going on with you best?"

"Shit my bored ass just got back from my day job. What you been doing all day?"

"Nothing. I had to go out to Walmart. I seen Ant aggravating ass."

"What?" DeAsia was just as shocked as me. "What was his ass talkin' about? Who was he up der wit?"

"Man, I wish you was der. Talking about he couldn't even get a lunch date. He was trying to make me feel bad about not fuckin' with him, but he really gotta stop. It's been years, and for real when I started messing wit Jeez, we stopped communicating," I paused. "And he was pushin' up on me, I didn't even ask who he was in der wit, that bitch was packed."

"I hope you ain't fall into his bullshit, Mea. He had his chance, just like with Jeez. They decided to fuck wit the hoes. They fucked up. Carter stepped up and he's been nothing but real since day one, so that's who deserves you. Fuck everybody else.

Don't mess this up being dumb listening to dey bullshit!" DeAsia said, smacking her lips. "You got something good."

"You're right, and I didn't pay Ant any attention. I mean I gave him my number because we can be friends because I know Carter got friends, but I know I wouldn't take it no farther than that. He ain't got shit coming. I love Carter and he truly makes me happy," I explained.

"Good," she replied. "Plus, the fuck shit he pulled at the party from what I been hearing was on some corny shit. Ain't nobody on his shit. Den how the fuck is he tryin' to click with Carter and still tryin' to fuck with you. He a fuckin' weirdo, Mea, seriously. Leave that nigga alone. I'm just being honest best, nothing good is going to come from even talkin' to him."

I was silent for a moment. DeAsia was right, but then again she could be paranoid. I mean Ant knew how the game goes. I didn't give him any signs that I was going to fuck back with him. I think I made it very clear that I was happy with my bae. I looked at the time, I told DeAsia I would call her back. I needed to check in with Carter. I hadn't talked to him all day.

"La'Mea, if you don't listen to your best at least keep in mind that you just got out a rocky situation. This is something good. Don't allow your insecurities and past relationship to mess up what you have," DeAsia said before hanging up.

***

When I called Carter, he didn't answer. I decided to start dinner and hop in the shower. As I stood in the shower, I thought back to the night of the party. I knew for a fact that Ant was trying to get under Carter's skin when he said he got a good bitch on his team. Even though it was the truth, it was a nigga thing. He's an arrogant ass nigga. I shook my head and laughed to myself. He tried it, and I gave him an A for effort. Too bad the type of relationship me and Carter had couldn't be broken over that type of bullshit. I was so caught up in my thoughts, I never heard Carter come in.

"Damn bae yo thick ass!" he said, opening the shower curtain.

“Hey bae. I missed you.” I stuck my head out the shower for a kiss.

Carter kissed me three times in a row as he undressed and joined me in the shower. I had never took a shower with a nigga before. I was a little nervous; I placed my arms across my chest as he stepped in. Carter stood in front of me allowing the water to run down his back. I never did a lot of stuff sexually, and I didn’t mind trying new things as long as it was with him.

“Relax, bae. It’s not like I never seen you naked before.” He pulled me close to him and kissed me again. “Act like this ain’t even a shower. Close your eyes and relax.”

I did as I was told. I closed my eyes and took a deep breath. Although he told me to pretend that we were not in the shower, a part of me was still tense. I let out a sigh.

“Are you cool?” he asked.

I nodded.

I reached down and stroked his dick. I closed my eyes again and pretended we were lying in the bed. I dropped to my knees to kiss and play with his dick, after a few kisses and licks it was hard as a rock. I wrapped my lips around the head. I allowed my tongue to go around the tip. I took him deep in my throat. The water made my mouth wetter than normal. I loved sucking his dick as much as he loved getting his dick sucked. I begin deep throating his dick hard, taking him deep down my throat. I sucked harder and harder, pausing for a second allowing his dick to sit in my throat. I felt him buckle on the wall.

“Damn bae,” I heard him moan.

I continued; I didn’t stop. He motioned for me to stand up. We changed positions and now I was under the shower. I arched my back as he slid inside me. I let out a slight moan. A chill ran down my spine. Hitting me from the back, he reached up and grabbed my breast.

“Oh bae!” I cried out. “Umm!”

“You missed me?”

“Yes,” I uttered. “Oh, bae. I missed you!”

He continued to hit me from the back. Throwing my ass

back, I grinded to the motion of his dick. I loved feeling him inside me. I felt him reach up and turn off the water. We stepped out and he bent me over the sink and continued to fuck me.

"Throw that shit back bae," he ordered.

I did as I was told again, I could hardly catch my breathe. I started to lose count after the first three times I came. After he came, we both got back in the shower and enjoyed each other's company. I loved when Carter was at home. It was never a dull moment, between playing the game, or breaking out the board games, we always had a good time. We laid in the bed and he started playing Fortnite.

"Bae, have you ever thought about doing something different?"

"What you mean, bae?" he asked, still concentrating on killing the zombies.

"Like you know, like getting a regular job?"

He paused the game and looked at me strange.

"What's with all the questions?" he asked confused.

"I was just asking; I mean we always talk about things we would like to do. I know once I finish school, I'm going to apply for University."

"Well, you already know I'm not going to be doing this shit too much longer. I just wanna make enough so I can live comfortably," he replied as he started playing the game again.

"So, did you talk to Ant?"

Carter quickly paused the game again and glared at me. From the look on his face, I already knew he was about to say some smart shit. I looked at the floor and started playing with my feet.

"Why?"

"Well I know at your party you said he was asking about some business, so I was just curious." I tried to make myself sound so innocent.

"Yeah okay, nah doe, I'm not fuckin' wit it. That nigga just got outta jail. I don't need that type of heat on us. Plus, he was in the Feds too. I'm cool. He can go get business from somewhere else." He looked me up and down. "So, what's the story behind ya'll anyway?"

"We used to talk back in the day before he went to jail, but it wasn't nothing like I was his main bitch or nothing. Don't get me wrong I fucked with him heavy. But shit changed after he went to jail. Everything that goes on in the dark comes to light, that shit is true as fuck. So, I just completely stop fuckin' with him," I admitted truthfully. "We didn't work, I moved on. That's about it."

"Oh yeah," he said.

I looked at him. He hit with the 'oh yeah' like I was lying or something. I wanted to continue and really stress that the shit was nothing now, but it was no use; Carter knew that I was solid. I've been nothing but loyal to him since day one. I wasn't trying to fuck up what we had.

"Bae, don't say *oh yeah* like that. I'm serious," I whined.

"Shut up, crybaby. I'm not thinking about that shit. You already know I will kick yo ass if it's anything other den that. We good. I just wanted to know."

I smiled. I couldn't help but love him even more. We communicated and kept shit on the table, so it was never any confusion. I laid my head on Carter's lap and watched him play the game. The urge to play with his dick was so hard to resist. I was definitely ready for round two.

***

The next few days, I barely got to see my bae. I had moved to second shift, and he was in and out of town making moves with his brothers. I felt bae sick. I hated being home alone. I wanted to just come home, cuddle, and tell him about my day. I think that's what I hated the most about the street life. It was so different from being with Jeez. We were together all the time, except when I was at work, or unless he was doing some slick shit with some hoes. I looked at my phone and sent him a text.

Hey Bae, I miss you. When are you coming to the house?

I watched the message send and say delivered. I loved that most about the Iphone's and I knew when he read the message too. I really didn't want nothing more but for him to come home and fuck the shit out of me and cuddle. My spoiled ass needed some attention. Moments later, I heard Carter's ringtone.

I miss you too love. I got some more running around to do, I should be home late tonight. I will wake you when I get der.

I wanted to complain, but I just told him okay and laid across the bed. I knew I had my ways to get him home quicker, especially telling him how I wanted to suck his dick with a fruit roll up. I laughed to myself.

Carter

Making money was something I liked doing. Shit, I loved expensive shit, so I had to get out there and get it. Being a fly nigga wasn't cheap. Half the niggas out here were really faking it, rocking fake shit, playing the role. In reality, my brothers and I was really living that lifestyle. We started from nickels and dimes to being them niggas. Don't get me wrong, I wanted to get out the game eventually. Maybe even get a factory job, but first I needed to make at least one hundred thousand or better. Shit I just want to live good and settle down eventually. Right now, I was just enjoying life, I loved this shit; the money, clothes, cars, and hoes. I mean I had it. I invested my time in a few females, but it was nothing major just really something to do.

I looked at my phone, I noticed my bae, La'Mea, had texted me. She wasn't my normal bitch I would fuck with. She was on the average side. She had been down and loyal since I started fucking with her, plus she had some good pussy, so I was fucking with her. She definitely had showed me another side of her when she threw me the birthday party at The Bank.

I was out running around; we had a shipment that came in that required my brother and I to be at the spot together for a few days. Business was good and I couldn't complain. We kept shit at a low profile because we didn't need the bullshit. I noticed I missed a call; I was trying to get shit done, but business was business.

"What up somebody call Carter?"

"Yeah, what up my nigga. I'm tryin to link to talk about that business I had in mind," an unfamiliar voice replied. "Put me on."

"Shit, who is this?" I asked. I didn't have time for the weird shit people be on.

"Ant, Shawn introduced us at your birthday party," he said still gassed up.

"Oh yeah, what's up?" I still didn't know what he was getting at.

"Shit, I'm tryin' to get back out here. Throw ya nigga a pack or something."

"Man, I'm not even gon' lie to you, I'm just not feeling it. You just got out the Feds, brah. You need to sit down and wait a minute before you jump back in the game. My brothers and I don't need that unnecessary heat on us right now," I paused for a moment. "Maybe another time?"

It was silent for a second. I looked at my phone to check if he was still there.

"Man, if you worried about the pigs watching me, don't be. I did my time, and I'm free. No probation or nothing my nigga. I'm just trying to get out here and make this money. I'm not trying to cause problems for you and your people, brah," Ant broke the silence.

"I just don't have any business for you right now, brah," I repeated. "We good right now, if anything come up, I will hit up back."

"Bet my nigga," Ant said before hanging up.

I looked at my phone again and shook my head. I just wasn't feeling that nigga. He blew me that day talking about I had a good bitch on my team. Just the fact that he was fucking my bitch, and wanted me to put him on was slow. I mean what type of fuck nigga did he take me for.

***

My brothers left early to run some errands, while I stayed behind waiting on the business to come through. I reached for my phone as someone knocked on the door. It was like a never ending thing. I really shouldn't have gotten comfortable, already knowing how this shit was about to go, plus it was the first of the month.

"Yo, yo," I said as I opened the door, not knowing who it

was.

"Hey daddy," Monea smiled as she pushed passed me. "What's up with you?"

"Shit, how you get over this way?" I asked surprised to see her.

"I thought I would drop by and check on you since you ain't been to the house to feel on my fat ass, and give me some dick," she replied, licking her lips.

"Oh yeah?" I smirked. "I've been busy doe real shit. Business been kinda crazy, so it's been requiring my full attention."

"Tell me anything." She rolled her eyes.

I met Monea the summer of last year in the club. She was a stripper, but she stayed in all the hottest spots. She was short and light skinned with a fat ass. Every nigga in the club wanted to be able to take her home. I guess it was just my turn and lucky me. She was cool; I fucked with shawty. I grabbed her and pulled her close to me. She stuck her tongue out as she kissed my lips. Baby girl was a freak on top of everything.

"Come on, daddy. Fuck this pussy," she said, slowly taking off her clothes.

I took off my watch and placed it on the side of the tv. I looked up again and she was completely undressed. I watched her play with her fingers with her tongue, then gently rub them across her clit. She grabbed my hands and guided me to the back bedroom. Mounted on all fours she was ready for every inch of this dick I was going to give her. I wiggled her ass as she threw her ass back.

"Oh daddy, fuck this pussy!"

I slapped her on the ass as I continued to fuck her. I could feel myself about to cum, I pulled out and busted all on her back. A nigga wasn't trying to have any extra kids no time soon. My two boys were enough right now.

I stood in the bathroom wiping my dick off. I knew Monea was still in the room, probably doing some shit that would piss me off. I walked back into the room, Monea jumped and dropped my phone. I just shook my head. It never fails, she was always in my shit.

"You know I hate when you go through my shit, man. Why do you keep doing it?" I tossed her the towel so she could wipe herself off.

"You haven't been with me, so I wanted to know what you been doing my nigga. You talkin' about the business been taking your full attention, but from what I see in your phone is telling me something else." Monea threw the towel back at me.

"Man, stop going through my shit, man. That's not cool. I hate that shit." I grabbed my clothes and started getting dressed.

"So, you not gon' explain what's in your phone?" Monea stormed behind me.

I just shook my head. I didn't have to for real. I mean the pussy was good, but I didn't have time for her to get on my nerves. If anything, I had to deal with the shit when I went home because I already knew La'Mea was waiting to complain about me being gone all day.

"Man, you gotta ride back to where you're going? My brothers are about to be on their way back, and we gotta go make some plays," I said, completely changing the subject.

"Don't do that shit, Carter. I asked you a question." She pushed me slightly.

"And I asked you a question. I don't have time for this bull-shit. We can talk about this later. I will come by the house or something."

She knew I was lying because I hadn't been coming through on none of the plans I've been making, but I really didn't wanna be bothered with her interrogating bullshit right now.

"Yeah, I'm good. Just call me when you're about to come by the house," she replied as she stormed out the door.

The bullshit I had been getting myself into lately was unreal. I sat back in the chair and turned back on the PS4.

***

I loved the smell of food when I walked in the house. My plate was sitting on the kitchen table wrapped up so nicely. Bae had definitely put it down in the kitchen with steak, shrimp, baked potato, and broccoli with cheese. I placed my plate in the microwave to warm it up as I looked around at the rest of the downstairs. She had also changed everything around. I shook my head and laughed. I never really had to worry about Mea getting bored with sitting in the house when I was away because she always found something to do, rather it was to clean up the house or to change some shit around. Every other day our bedroom would be changed into a different angle. I grabbed my food and headed to the room.

"Bae, wake up," I yelled, sitting on my side of the bed. "Come eat with me."

She rolled over and glared at me. I just knew her ass was about to be on some bullshit.

"Bae, you're gonna make me fat den you're not going to want me no more," she busted out laughing.

"Shut the fuck up and get over here and eat with me. Nobody told yo ass to eat without me anyway," I said kissing her once she sat up. "Now you gotta eat twice and imma always want you. You just gone be my fat butter ball."

We both laughed. I said the prayers over the food and searched for something to watch as we ate. I looked over at her and she was so gorgeous. It really didn't matter what she had on, my baby was sexy as hell. She really didn't care about looking rough and she always thought my rough look was so sexy anyway.

"What bae?" she said, stuffing another shrimp in her mouth.

"Nothing, you're just so fuckin' sexy."

"Gone, bae. I look a hot mess with this bonnet on. I probably got all types of stuff on my mouth," she complained.

"Shut up, bae!"

After we finished eating, I watched her collect all the mess and run it downstairs. I looked at her hips and her ass. My baby was getting thick as fuck. She wasn't missing any meals. I laughed to myself.

"So how is everything going? How was work today?" she asked as I laid my head on her lap.

I loved when she brushed and played with my hair. If it wasn't my hair or my beard, it was her tracing my tattoos and massaging me. She always wanted to just cater to me.

"Same ol, same ol, bae. You know how this shit be. Yo boy called me today!"

"My boy who?" she instantly stopped playing in my hair.

"Yo nigga!" I said sarcastically.

"Stop playing with me." She gently pushed my head forward.

"Don't do that shit again, lil fat girl. And you know that's yo nigga." I laughed again.

"No, my nigga is about to get fucked up if he keeps playing with me like this," she said trying to get up.

"Shut up, crybaby. I know that ain't yo nigga. But he did call."

"And so, did you tell him that you were cool on that business shit?"

"Yeah I did. I don't think he was too happy about the answer I gave him, but that nigga will be alright." I shrugged.

"Good, I don't think ya'll shoulda worked together anyway. Bae, ya'll in the zone and that woulda been a distraction. I just know how they operate," she replied as she started to run her fingers through my beard. "I missed you. You been gone working hard and shit!"

"I miss you more, baby. You trying to put me together or nah."

She looked me up and down for a moment and slid her hands down my chest. She was fascinated with all my tattoos, even though she's seen them a hundred times she found something new about them each time she touched them. She slid down and pulled out my dick that was nearly on hard and kissed the tip of the head. She loved playing with my dick. She continued to kiss and lick the head. She took me deep in her throat. She sucked my dick like it was going to be her last time.

"Damn." I moved trying to reposition myself.

She continued to suck my dick; her mouth was wet as fuck.

Her gag reflex was everything, twisting both her hands round my dick, her two-hand combo had my eyes rolling in the back of my head. I motioned for her to come up. She climbed on top and started riding me. She wasn't playing any games.

"Oh shit." I pulled her down. "Damn, bae."

She laid on her side and I began stroking her slow. I listened to her let out a faint moan. I wrapped my hands around her neck and started fucking her even harder. She gripped the sheets as I continued to fuck her.

"Oh bae," she called out.

"Tell me when you're about to cum on this dick," I demanded.

"Bae," she cried out again, trying to push me back, but I didn't budge. I fucked her even harder.

"Oh bae, I'm about to cum."

Just as she came, I came too. I knew that wasn't a good idea considering she still hadn't come on her monthly cycle. I kept up with her period like it was my own. I wanted to mention it, but it could have changed. She got up and grabbed the towel out the bathroom, and returned so she could wipe me down. I watched her climb back in bed. I wrapped my arms around her. I don't know if she knew how much I really loved her. It felt so good when we're together.

***

The next day, I decided to grab my boys and spend some time with them. It had been about two weeks since I last got them. When I pulled up both of them was playing in the front yard. Dameir and Rio ran up to the car as soon as I pulled in the driveway good. Even though they were two years apart you really couldn't tell. Dameir had just turned seven and Rio was five. I loved my boys. They were one of the reasons I grinded so hard. I wanted them to have everything that I didn't have. I didn't want them to want for shit.

"Daddy, are we coming with you?" Rio asked opening the passenger door. "I wanna go with you."

"Me too," Dameir chimed in.

I looked at both of them and smiled.

"Yeah, go grab ya'll stuff, and bring your game so ya'll can play," I said, turning off the car. "Is your mother in there?"

"No, she ran to the store, my gma in the house cooking some food!" Rio yelled as he ran towards the house. "Can we go to the mall again?"

I looked at him and laughed again. They really thought I was a walking bank. I was kind of happy their mother was gone; I didn't have time to hear all her shit. Lately, she had been on some other shit. I wasn't feeling it at all. I just wanted to spend time with my boys. When I walked in, I sat on the couch waiting on them to come back downstairs.

"Dad, is we going swimming?" Rio yelled from the top of the stairs.

"Do ya'll wanna go swimming?" I leaned over the side of the couch so I could see him.

"Yeah, we do," Dameir chimed in.

I smiled and Rio ran back to his room to finish getting ready. I started to go up there and make sure they grabbed some reasonable stuff, and wasn't looking crazy but I'm pretty sure they would be cool. After five minutes, the boys ran back past me to say goodbye to their grandmother and we were on our way out.

***

"So, what do ya'll wanna do first?" I asked as we jumped on the highway. "Did ya'll eat?" They both shook their heads no. I knew they were lying. If it was one thing their grandma always did, she made sure they ate, and had snacks all day. I looked at both of them again.

"Well how about we go to the hotel so ya'll can swim, we can order a pizza, and stop at the store to get some junk food."

They both smiled at the idea. I was going home, but I could just call La'Mea and tell her to meet us at the hotel. They wanted to swim, and it would be nice to get out the house. I reached for my phone and called my bae.

"What's up beautiful."

"Hey baby. What's up?" she answered on the first ring.

"Where are you, love?"

"About to be on my way home," she paused.

I heard a lady say La'Mea's last name. I tried to listen, but she must have put the phone on mute.

"La'Mea!" I called out to her. "Hey Love?"

"My bad, baby. I'm about to go home," she repeated herself. "Where are you? Did you get the boys?"

"Yeah, I thought you was at work?" I was now confused.

"I was, I had an accident at work, but I'm okay," she replied.

"Are you sure, love," I was now concerned, and was wondering why she didn't call me when it first happened.

"Yes, just feel a little lightheaded, but I'm okay. It's nothing," she paused again. "So, what's up, baby."

"Well, I was calling to see if you could pick up a pizza and come up to the hotel. The boys wanna swim and it would be nice just to get out the house."

"Okay, I can do that. Let me run home and change out of my uniform and I will be on my way. Is it something you need from the house?"

"Yeah, just my wave cap, my basketball shorts, my Polo jogging suit, a pair of boxers, and a pair of socks," I replied, trying to make sure I named everything.

"Okay Carter, I will call you when I'm on my way. I love you," she said before hanging up.

"I love you too."

***

Two hours passed, we were settled in our room, and Mea had made it. We decided to head down to the pool to swim.

"So can ya'll swim because I know for sure that yo daddy can't swim," La'Mea laughed.

"I can swim!" the boys yelled at the same time.

"Okay, don't be holding on to the wall," she laughed again.

"Don't be talking about me, bae," I said, pushing her playfully.

"It's okay. I still love you," she laughed even harder while trying to kiss me.

It felt good to have my woman and boys together. We laughed and joked all night. Even though I wanted to press the issue about Mea not feeling well, I didn't want to spoil the moment. We could talk about it later. I loved having the opportunity to spend time with my boys.

***

Monday morning, it was a regular scheduled day for me. Breakfast, the gym, and meet my brothers for our weekly meeting. We needed to touch bases about a few things. This Monday, Mea and I didn't ride together. Plus, I had to drop the boys off at school. She seemed really tired though, so I knew she didn't want to run around with me and go to the gym like we would normally do. When I got to the hood, my brothers were already there stuck in front of the video game.

"Yo ass always late," Cartier uttered as I walked through the door.

"I'm just coming from the gym and dropping the boys off." I grabbed a chair and pulled it next to theirs. "It's been busy today?"

"Nah, not really. It's the normal crowd," Cartier mumbled. "It's Monday. Yo regulars came through already before work. You know your clientele."

"So, what ya'll think about opening up a club?" Ced asked, focused on the game.

"Where at?" I asked, leaning back in the chair. "I mean I was thinkin' about something more lowkey, like some buildings or shit a store in the hood. You know niggas will fuck with us no matter what. I know a few places that's been closed down that we could get our hands on or even copping some house, something legit."

"I mean just something to fall back on. You know mommy was just saying she wouldn't mind putting some shit in her name for us. So, we would have somewhere to make your money clean. It's not a bad idea," Cartier added. "We don't need no extra heat, especially if we're planning to give this shit up for good."

"Yeah, that's a good idea. I mean we been on some lowkey

shit doe. Like that shit other hoods and shit go through be too much." Ced shook his head.

"Yeah, speaking of that, ya'll heard about that bullshit that was going on with Shawn and dem niggas beefing like crazy." I mentioned.

"Yeah, that's the bullshit we don't need. We got families, and I don't wanna put anybody in any unnecessary bullshit," Ced replied, pausing the game. "If we gone get out the game we gon' do it right."

"Yeah, that's why I told the nigga, Ant, we are good on him. He wanted me to put him on," I started to explain. "This nigga just got out the feds. We didn't have time for that shit."

"Where did he come from?" Cartier asked.

"He came with the nigga Shawn the night of my party," I said.

I left out the fact that La'Mea used to fuck with him. That shit still didn't sit well with me. I wasn't planning to do any business with him so anything else about him didn't matter. We finished up with our business meeting, and I decided to chill. I noticed that I had a missed call from an unknown number. My phone started ringing again. I was hesitant at first, I got up and walked into the kitchen.

"Hello," I finally answered.

"Hi, is this Carter Smith?" a lady asked.

"Yes, may I ask who's calling."

"Hi, my name is Dr. Smooth, I'm La'Mea Morgan's doctor, she had told me just in case of emergency that I could get in touch with you," she explained.

"Yes, is this about her accident at work," I asked confused because what this emergency could be about.

"Yes, Mr. Smith, so she did inform you about what's going on?" she asked.

"Yes, basically," I lied.

"Well, her test results we gave her about the pregnancy was confirmed, and she is very much pregnant from her blood test but we also have a concern about her levels of iron being extremely low, that may have been one of the reason she passed out at work, on top of her being dehydrated." She continued.

"So, when does she need to come back?" I asked with concern.

"I have made her an appointment for Thursday. I also left her a message about it explaining she needed to make sure she made it to the appointment," she replied.

"Okay, Dr. Smooth, I will make sure she makes it," I assured her before hanging up.

I was so confused. Why didn't she mention to me that she found out she was pregnant.

Jeez

This jail shit was really taking a toll on me. It seemed like niggas got in here and changed up. The same niggas I considered my brothers, my family left me for dead. Loyalty was just a tattoo and some shit that sounded good at the moment. These niggas didn't have a clue what loyalty was. I was still standing ten toes down; niggas couldn't pay me to be a rat. I always stood behind the fact it wasn't what you know, it was what you could prove. I've never been fooled; I knew how the game went. Plus, my lawyer was such a fucking animal in the court room, I really didn't have any worries.

Today I was in a real good mood. My brother, Shawn, and my mom were coming to see me. I knew my mother was going through a lot, I had just promised her this was the last time being in this situation. Now look at me, I was sitting down in the county jail awaiting trial.

"Aye Robertson, it's time for your visit," the CO called from the doorway of my cell.

I nodded to him and hopped off my bunk. For me to be in jail, a nigga wasn't really losing sleep. I was getting my weight up and basically chilling. Don't get me wrong, I would love to be in the streets, but shit I was to the point where it is what it is. This was just a temporary situation. I walked slowly through the doors. They greeted me at a small round table, and I got to hug them for a brief moment.

"You look good, baby," my mom said, smiling. "I miss you."

"I miss you too, ma." I grabbed her hands and held them in mine. "I'm so sorry, ma. You shouldn't have to go through this again. But trust this will be over soon. I promise."

"How are you holding up? Have you spoken to your lawyer? What's going on with your case now?" Shawn came with the questions.

"Well, so far he said they really don't have shit on me but a bunch of hearsay. That really don't hold any weight. Niggas just talkin' with no real evidence." I shrugged. "I'm learning these niggas some bitches."

"Jesus, I just want you to leave this lifestyle alone. I don't want any of my kids in this place," my momma said, interrupting us.

"I know, ma. I promise, this shit is going to be over before you know it. Imma be back home and this time imma find a job and shit. You gonna see." I tried to sound as convincing as possible.

"So have you talked to that hoe Bri?" Shawn continued with his questions.

"Man, hell nah. That hoe definitely had something to do with them coming to pick me up. I know that for sure." I was pissed all over again. "Have you talked to La'Mea?"

Shawn's eyes got big and then he looked at the table. I knew something wasn't right. I was afraid to ask, but I missed her big head ass. I hadn't heard from her since I last did a three-way call and asked her to look out for me.

"Shawn."

"Man, she fuck with that nigga Carter!" he finally looked up at me.

"Carter?" I paused and thought for a moment. "The nigga I beat her ass about?"

"It gotta be. You know that nigga up the way. Him and his brothers got a cold connect. I introduced Ant and Carter the night of his party, that's where I found out about him and Mea," he mumbled.

"Damn," I dropped my head. "So ya'll ain't seen her since then?"

Shawn shook his head no. I never thought I would hear that she really moved on. She hadn't written me or nothing. Out of all people I would have never thought she would have left me for dead in here. I mean yeah she dropped a few dollars but damn, she was giving my pussy away like the shit was cool. I thought I fucked her up enough she wouldn't even talk to any nigga name Carter. Dirty ass disloyal bitch.

"I mean Ant want parts in their business, and you know Mea used to be fuckin' with him a while back and he said he wants his spot back. He wants his bitch back too," Shawn added.

I gave him a blank stare. I didn't give a fuck about none of that shit. La'Mea was my bitch. All these niggas thought it was just cool to be plotting on her. I had a feeling some fuck shit was going to happen once I got in this position. I placed my head in my hands. I wanted to punch some shit right now.

"Man, it's about that time man. Brah, imma holla at you," I said, standing up motioning for the CO. "Make sure ya'll put some money on ya'll phone. I love ya'll."

On my way back to cell, I asked the CO for a phone call. I had to call her. At first I was going to wait and collect my thoughts, but I was pissed the fuck off. I couldn't believe this bitch was out here living life, messing with niggas, like she didn't know what it was. I don't give a fuck what the circumstances were, she was my bitch. I dialed her number and took a deep breath.

"Hello," I heard her say as the recording played. I paused for a second, I didn't know if she was going to accept my call or not.

"La'Mea," I finally spoke up. "Are you there?"

"What's up, Jeez," she sounded like she was half sleep.

"Don't what's up me, my nigga. The fuck you don't know what loyalty is no more, huh?"

She sucked her teeth and let out a loud sigh.

"You know I hate that shit! Don't do that shit while I'm talking to you. Don't suck your fucking teeth!" I yelled through the phone. "So, you out here fuckin' with these fuck niggas, huh?"

"Jeez, what I do is not your concern. I'm not your bitch! Ain't that the shit you kept yelling, always talking about I wasn't your girl. Stand on that shit now!" she replied with an attitude. "Who I'm fuckin' is not your business. Now what is that you want?"

"Bitch, what you mean? Hoe you could be in the same place I am right now. What the fuck are you talking about? That innocent role you're playing, you can cut the shit. Bitch, you out here fuckin' da same nigga I beat yo ass about like it's cool." I was pissed. She had me all the way fucked up. "Bitch, yo ass need to be holding me down like a loyal bitch, but no you're out running around like a disloyal ass hoe."

I didn't give a fuck at this point about La'Mea or her feelings. She had me fucked up. I couldn't believe her. Out of all the niggas she could have been fucking, she goes back to a nigga she tried to embarrass me with. What the fuck was she thinking? I mean really. I don't know if it was a good thing I was in here or not, but I knew one thing for certain and two things for sure if I wasn't, I would be in this bitch for murder for real. I would have been ripped Mea's head off and waited for the police to show up.

"Jeez, I don't even know why you're so mad. You played me, you dogged me, you lied to me for so long. Now you wanna feel a certain kinda way because I moved on. You created this. I was holding you down. You know me. You know when I'm fuckin' with one person, I'm only fuckin' with that person. You know my loyalty and what that means to me. You had me; I was right there for so long until I realized that I was the only one in love in our relationship!" she yelled through the phone. "SO, IF YOU WANNA BLAME ANYBODY FOR LOSING YOUR BITCH, BLAME YOURSELF, JESUS ROBERTSON!"

The call ended moments later. I wanted to call back just for her reaction. I know I fucked her head up when I said that nigga's government name. See, I had did my own research on the nigga when I found out who she had fucked behind my back. Carter was a lot like me, money motivated and he had them hoes. I mean, I knew a few hoes that still had some dealings with him including his baby mother. I didn't know him personally, but I knew some niggas that did. If La'Mea thought she was moving on to something better, she only was moving on to someone who was probably doing her the same way she felt I did her, maybe even worse.

The only difference will be that he probably hides it a lot better than me. Shit, I'm not hiding shit nor locking shit or nothing. I showed La'Mea every time that I didn't want to lose her, so for her to jump ship was disloyal.

I walked to my cell still not feeling like I got everything off my chest. I wanted to call back and argue some more. I wanted to get through to her that I expected a lot more from her. She was supposed to be my rider. I never imagined a day that I would look up and the person I loved would be gone. My bunkie was still in the yard. I hopped on my bed and laid there looking at the ceiling. I wasn't sure how I was going to get through this trial without her. I never thought I would have to. Forever is never really forever. My bitch switched up on me just like my niggas did.

Ant

Being a free man was something that didn't take too much time to get used to. I didn't have no more lock downs, counts; a nigga ate, shit, and slept when the fuck he wanted to now. It felt good to see La'Mea. I swear I missed her so much. I wanted to tell her I thought when I got out it would be me and her. But the first day I got out and she wasn't with King and them when I walked out those gates was a major disappointment. Shit, I should've known when the letters and pictures kept coming up short. I was out here now. I was ready to get back what was mine. This was my city. I ran these streets. I pulled up in the hood and everybody was out.

"Brah, what's up," I said, dapping everybody up.

"Where yo ass been at?" King asked, passing me the other half of his Newport.

"Man, you know I had to do my daddy thing before I came out to run the streets." I smiled.

It felt good to be able to spend time with my kids, and not be placed on a time limit and shit like that. That was the reason, I wanted to get this money, so I could do more for them. They deserved to have the best and neither one of their mothers could get the type of money that I was capable of making. Before I left it wasn't nothing that my kids didn't have rather it was a want or a need. I made shit happen, I was that nigga. Shit I made sure I looked out for everybody, not just for family either.I always gave back; I was never a stingy nigga.

"So, did you link with that nigga Carter yet?" Shawn asked, coming out the trap.

"I was actually gon' give that nigga a call today since he

didn't make it his business to get back to me," I replied going through my phone. "We definitely need to put this play down to get shit back up and running. How was brah when you went to see him?"

"I mean he's holding up. He didn't say much, I know he really just got a lot on his mind being in this situation and all."

"I know it's fucked up. We definitely gon' make shit work so whatever the outcome is, we get him together," I assured him. "We family, that's what we do."

"I already know." He dapped me up.

I lowkey had an issue with him fucking with La'Mea, but I couldn't be mad; he was always going to be my nigga. It wasn't his fault she gave my pussy away to him. I mean as much as I love her ass, she was going to pay for embarrassing me.

***

After the first conversation, Carter made it clear that he didn't wanna do business with me. That shit made me feel a certain kinda way, not only did he have my bitch, but he was the plug. I started to think maybe Shawn shouldn't have mentioned that I was in the feds, but it wasn't like I was on parole or something. I was free to go. No probation, no check ins; I did my time and I was done with that shit. I was so pissed off, and I knew my niggas would be too. We all were counting on this play to put us back on. I looked at my phone and decided to go to happy hour downtown. I needed a drink.

***

When I walked in, it was ass everywhere. I sat at the bar and ordered a double shot of Absolute. I needed a few of these just to get my mind right. How was I going to explain this to my niggas. This nigga just brushed me off, like it would be a problem working with me. I placed my head in my hands. I was addicted to the fast money; I couldn't see myself grinding for no pennies working a nine to five. That shit just wouldn't work for me.

When I looked up, I noticed a short, yellow bone female standing in the corner. She was pretty as hell. When she turned around, her ass was so fat and juicy, I almost lost my train of thought. I ordered me another drink and headed over to get me a better look.

"Hey, how you doin'?" I asked, tapping her shoulder.

"Hey," she said and smiled.

"I hope I'm not interrupting you or bothering you."

"Nah, what's up? Did you need something?"

"You work here? What's your name?"

"Yes, I normally work the parties at night, but today I just need the extra money, and my name is Monea," she smiled again.

"If you were my girl, I would never make you work in a place like this!" I looked around once more. "A girl like you is to be kept, spoiled, and treated like a queen."

"Not a lot of MEN, can handle that type of responsibility. I'm not your normal kept female. I have my wants and needs, and they all need to be met." She licked her lips seductively.

I knew what type of female she was, but hey I wasn't really looking to wife no bitch. I had my wife already, I just needed to get her back.

"So where is yo man at? I know he ain't let you in here working and nowhere close by just in case some shit jumps off," I said, fishing for answers.

"Tah, I don't think my man wants the job anymore, he's been occupied with other business, I guess. Whatever the fuck that means." She rolled her eyes. "Where's your girl at?"

I knew it was coming.

"Well, she left me back when I was doing my bid up state," I lied. "I don't need no girl like that. Plus, I heard she was fuckin' around with a few niggas so I don't want her back."

It sounded real good. I mean the story was kind of farfetched, but it worked and from the looks of it she was buying every piece of it.

"So, what kinda work do you do?"

"I work in a factory and I got my side hustle," I lied again, shit not like she was the police doing a background check on a nigga. "So, you should let me take you out or something."

"I mean that sounds nice. What did you have in mind?" she asked, leaning in towards me.

"I mean dinner or a movie. What do you do for fun?" I asked. "I just wanna get to know you."

She smiled and we talked for a while before we exchanged numbers. Baby girl alright. I was really trying to see what that little shit was hitting for. I watched her work the floor. She did her thang; it was funny because she caught me a few times watching her. I got another drink and headed for the door; I had a lot on my mind and the liquor wasn't doing shit, but adding fuel to the fire. I needed a new plug and I needed to get back in the game. It's so fucked up because I normally had a plan b, but I was sure this shit was going to go through.

***

I walked in my mom's house and everybody was sitting in the living room, playing Grand Theft Auto. I dapped everybody up and sat in the corner, and lit a Newport 100.

"So, I talked to that bitch ass nigga Carter," I paused to make sure I had everybody's attention. "That nigga said he ain't fuckin' wit it. Talkin' about I just got out and he don't need that type of heat."

"Man, get the fuck outta here!" Shawn yelled. "Them niggas act like they couldn't front you a brick. That shit is crazy as fuck."

"That's that bullshit." King sat back and lit a blunt. "So that's the reason he gave you? Or is it because you were fuckin his bitch first."

"Shit, I don't know. If it was over that bitch, that nigga really a bitch ass nigga. And when did they get together anyway," I asked curious.

"Shit, she cheated on Jeez," Shawn replied. "Jeez and Mea went to blows because that was the nigga she left the bar with one night."

"Wait, La'Mea cheated?" I was surprised because Mea lived by that loyalty shit.

"I mean ya'll can't say that because La'Mea and Jeez wasn't official no matter how much they was fucking with each other. You know Jeez would tell niggas and her quick that she wasn't his bitch," Darnell explained.

"Stop takin' up for her ass. She knew how the game went," King interrupted. "Shit, the stuff she was pulling you couldn't tell me they wasn't in a relationship. She busted my nigga's car windows out, they was living together, and my nigga beat her ass for fuckin' with that nigga Carter. Y'all know how the game go. They was together, ain't no way you could convince me otherwise."

"Yeah, King gotta point," Shawn agreed. "Jeez was heated when I told him who she was fuckin' with."

"That shit don't mean nothing for real. I know one thing; we definitely need a new plug man. We all got families, we gotta get it," Dezmond interrupted.

"I say we rob that nigga, shit that nigga don't wanna put us on, its only right. We tried to get money with him and that nigga didn't wanna do that." King shrugged.

"Shit, we can do that too. Catch that nigga slippin', I mean that's normally how the game go anyway," I agreed. "We just need to start watching how he move."

"Ya'll think Mea will be any help?" Dezmond questioned.

"I mean, I really don't know. She don't act the same for real," Ant said with a smirk.

"We don't need her. We just gotta be patient. Trust something will come about." Shawn sat back in his chair.

Shawn was right, shit had its own way of working itself out. Shit I just needed it to pull together quickly because niggas had families to take care. I didn't have time for the bullshit. I wanted to be back on top by all means necessary. Shit, a nigga was ready to live the good life, I wasn't used to no other lifestyle.

***

It had only been two days since I met Monea, and I found myself laid up with her. It didn't take me long at all. I knew after a few long talks on the phone, some dangerous flirting, and some promises we would be together. She was a straight freak too. I wasn't mad at all having to put in the work.

"What yo lil boyfriend gon' think about you cheating on him?" I asked sarcastically.

"Shit, we both cheating so I guess he won't be sayin' shit to me."

"So, what's the point in being together den? I mean you know you deserve better den just sharing a nigga," I uttered. "You gotta know your worth, Monea."

"I do, it's just that I benefit from him right now. He makes me financially stable; I can't just walk away and be out here fucked up. I have a daughter," she explained.

"By him?"

"Nah, but he has been there for me, and I do my share of bullshit. I be wanting to leave but it's an unstable situation."

"Well, whenever you're ready for something real, you let me know. You deserve the best." I kissed her on the forehead.

I watched her get up and walk to the bathroom. I looked around for my phone because I could hear it vibrating. I noticed that it wasn't my phone. Leaning over, I noticed it was Carter's name. What was the coincidence this was the same Carter. Moments later, I answered my own question when his face popped up on the screen when he called. I smiled to myself. I had my way in.

"Your phone was ringing." I smiled as she walked out the bathroom. "I didn't answer it doe."

"I didn't say nothing, it must have been him calling," she said, sitting on the edge of the bed.

"I didn't know Carter was your dude," I said trying to see how much information I could get out of her.

"Yeah, this is my first-time hearing from him since the last time I popped up on him at his spot." She rolled her eyes.

"Ya'll got in a fight? Did he put his hands on you or something?"

"No, I went through his phone and noticed he's been messing with some hoe name Mea or something. When I asked him about it, he basically blew me off." She sounded upset now.

"Look, I'm not no hatin' ass nigga, Imma tell you this, you deserve way fucking better. Trust me when I say this. That nigga, man," I paused for a moment. "Just know you deserve better; he's fucked up for not even keeping it real with you."

I knew I could say a lot of shit, but I had other plans. I needed to gain her trust, I wanted to know his ins and outs. She was my ticket. They said everything would fall in line. I could take Carter out when he least expected it, and have both of his bitches. I smiled to myself. I leaned over and kissed her lips.I had charm; I was capable of taking everything Carter had. I got caught up in my thoughts, I pushed her up on the bed, massaging her thighs, I began kissing her inner thighs. She was now dripping wet. I kissed pussy lips, and I heard her let out a moan. I was sucking and licking her clit; she slowly arched her back, and placed her hands on the back of my head.

"Oh my God." She tried to run. "Oh my God. I'm about to cum."

I pretended as if I didn't hear her. I paused and slid my dick into her wetness, just after my first two strokes she was already cumming. I didn't let up on her. I kept fucking her with no mercy. She was running from the dick.

"Don't run," I said, flipping her over, placing her on all fours.

I grabbed her hair and started hitting her from the back. She reached for the sheets. I loved fucking from the back. Monea was running at first, but started throwing that shit back. I could feel her cumming again.

Later that night, I watched her get dressed for work. The fitted dress showed every curve she had. I smiled at her; I didn't even notice when she looked over at me.

"What you over der smiling about?" she asked, now putting on her make-up.

"Yo sexy ass. Let's make this official. Be my girl."

"Stop playin' you know my situation." She rolled her eyes.

"What if I said I had a plan that would have us set for life. You wouldn't have to be out here in these clubs, and you can be the trophy wife you are," I said.

"What are you talkin' about, Ant? You don't even know me!" she sighed. "Plus, I told you I'm in a situationship."

"That nigga Carter? Man, he's playin' you. I didn't wanna say nothing, but he gotta whole other life he's living. He deals with you when he wants. He's with another bitch playin' house, and you know that!" I put the truth out there.

I watched the expression on her face, she knew I was telling the truth. She knew I wasn't lying. I didn't wanna say too much, just enough for her to get on my team.

"What are you trying to say?" she asked sitting next to me on the bed. "I mean really?"

"You know the truth, Monea. I don't have to spell it out to you! Everything that he has could be ours. The lifestyle, the money, we could be living. No more drama, you could be my wife. I know I don't know you, but baby we have all the time in the world. We can grow together." I paused. "Look, baby, all you gotta do is play your role, we can get him out the way."

She looked at the floor. Maybe I said too much because she walked away from me and it was an awkward silence. I wanted to follow after her, but a part of me thought I went too far.

"So, what exactly is your plan?" she asked as she emerged from the bathroom.

I was shocked. I didn't really have one right off the top of my head really. I just wanted Carter out the way.

"I don't wanna be a part of anything that's gonna hurt him. I mean, I know how the game goes so, I just don't wanna be a part of something that's gonna get anybody killed. Everybody takes a L at least once."

"I'm not talkin' about nobody getting killed, bae. I just want his connect and get put on that's all."

"So what? You're just gonna rob him and let him go?"

"We gon' just act like this was something at random. Maybe you can make him meet you somewhere, we rob him, scare him a little bit, and that's it. We get put on and that shit will be over and done with."

"I mean I just don't want him to get hurt that's all, I don't want no mistakes no accidents. Get the money and get out." Monea replied skeptical on the situation.

"Bae you know I wouldn't put you in a position to get fucked up. I just wanna get this money. We gon' be good, you can live like the queen you are."

Monea was silent for a moment, I kept trying to read the expressions on her face. I knew she cared about the nigga, but I also knew she was tired of the bullshit! She wanted to live like royalty, she was an expensive bitch. I knew I gave her an offer that she really couldn't pass up. She would be my trap queen.

"Okay, let me handle the getting him to the location. Ant, this shit gotta work out right and I don't want nothing falling back on me at all," she finally said. "And ya'll can't hurt him. I mean that or I won't have no parts."

I looked at her and I knew she was serious. All I needed was her to be onboard. I didn't really care about what she was talking about.

"I got you. Nothing's going to happen to that nigga!" I said sarcastically.

La'Mea

Life as I knew it was working out great. Carter and I was doing good. I had started a new job at University Medical. I would have never thought this would be my life. My first day at work was going great. I knew this would be an adjustment due to the fact I wasn't used to none of this. I finally found time to take a break; I sat down and I felt lightheaded. I placed my head in my hands. I knew I wasn't hungry; I cooked a nice breakfast before I left home, so I knew it wasn't that, my menstrual was late, it could have been changing. I needed something to drink. I stood up and collapsed to the floor.

When I woke up, my supervisor and head nurse was standing over me.

"How are you feeling, La'Mea?" the head nurse, Melissa, asked checking my vitals again.

"I don't know what happened. I was just fine, I got lightheaded out of nowhere." I looked at the IV in my arm. I had to think because this was my second time passing out like this. I had passed out at my old job too.

"Well we did some blood test; the results should be coming. You just relax, no working for you. Consider this your half a day," my supervisor Ciara smiled. "Melissa will come back and let you know something soon as we find out."

I nodded at her and smiled. I couldn't believe this was happening on my first day. I laid back and looked at the ceiling. I swear I hope it wasn't nothing crazy going on because fainting was serious. This reminded me of when I tried to kill myself and Jeez found me. I didn't think he would have been around after that, but shit he was a bigger nut than I was, he probably figured this bitch is crazy and I'm crazy too, shit we're a perfect fit. I laughed to myself. I kind of missed his punk ass. I rolled my eyes at the fact he called the other day to argue with me about messing with Carter. I already knew someone was going to go back and tell him, but I just didn't think he would spazz like that. Let him tell it I wasn't his bitch! This nigga was big mad. I shook my head and closed my eyes again.

Moments later, Melissa was knocking on the door.

"So, what's the verdict? Am I going to live?" I chuckled.

"Yeah, shit I lived so I know you're going to be fine!" she laughed too.

"So, what's up?" I asked. "Can I go?"

"Yes, you're just pregnant, honey!" She handed me the test results. "Is this your first pregnancy?"

I tuned her completely out. Pregnant? How far along? Wait, my period was late but not that damn late! I continued to read the results. How was I going to tell Carter? I mean we never discussed kids, and he already had the boys. How was I going to have a kid and I just started a new job.

"La'Mea?" Melissa called out. "Is this going to be your first pregnancy?"

"Oh yeah," I whispered.

"What's wrong? Why aren't you happy?" she questioned.

"I'm happy, it's not that. I just don't know how happy my boyfriend is going to be about it. We never talked about kids."

"But if ya'll fucking and I mean fucking without protection, you know it's a likely chance. These weak ass birth control methods ain't 100%." She sat at the edge of the bed. "You're a nurse girl, if that nigga don't wanna do the right thing, you got this. I do it by myself and I do a damn good job, honey."

"I just don't know how this shit is going to work, like I just started this job and everything. I'm not about to give up my job either," I confessed.

"You don't have to. See, you're looking at this from all the negatives. Girl, you can work and be pregnant. You're going to be fine." She stood up and begin taking my IVS out. "Setup a prenatal appointment, and an ultrasound. Then go home and take a warm bath, and relax. Everything is going to work itself out, trust me."

***

Sitting in the house wasn't part of my plans. I hadn't talked to Carter since I left the house this morning. I wanted to call him, but if I did I would have to tell him about me being pregnant, and that wasn't in my plans just yet. I wasn't trying to keep secrets because we didn't do that, but I wasn't ready. I decided to go to the mall; I found shopping as a type of therapy.

I loved Strongsville Mall, so I didn't mind taking the drive. I hit all my favorite stores: Victoria's Secret, Bath and Body Works, Beachwood Place, Claires, and H&M. As I was walking out of H&M, on my way to grab me something to eat, I heard someone say excuse me. I looked around and noticed a short, light skinned girl following me.

"Yes," I looked at my bags to see if I had dropped something. "Are you calling for me?"

"Ain't you Carter's girlfriend," Monea asked as she approached me.

"Yes, and you are?" I asked confused.

"So how long have ya'll been together?" she asked.

I was annoyed now. I didn't know this bitch, but she was asking a million questions like the fucking police. I didn't even answer her questions. Shit, I was still waiting on her to answer my question.

"Well, I hope ya'll work out. Considering what type of nigga he is," Monea laughed as she walked away.

I rolled my eyes. This little hoe was blowing me.

"Considering what type of nigga he is?" I mean what type of nigga was he? A street nigga? I shook my head, I didn't even notice my phone had started ringing.

"Hello," I answered, sounding irritated.

"Hey Ms. Anti," Ant said, laughing. "What's wrong with the big baby?"

I didn't have time for his shit today either. I didn't even

want to be bothered. I knew this was going to be a quick conversation.

"Ain't nothing wrong. What's up?" I tried to cut right to the point.

"I wanna see you."

"Now you know that's not gon' happen." I shot him right down. I wasn't in the mood. I could tell how the conversation was going he was just going to piss me off even more.

"Man, Mea stop acting like that towards me. We're supposed to be better den this. I just wanna talk to you about something," Ant pleaded.

"Okay, Ant. I answered my phone. You can talk now. Why do you have to see me?"

"If I wasn't for that nigga you're fucking, you wouldn't have time for me. You treat a nigga like me like shit," he complained.

"Ant, like seriously what do you want?" I was irritated.

"Man, I'm trying to keep you safe. Some shit is about to go down and I just want you to be aware, La'Mea."

"Like what doe?" I said frustrated.

"I can't talk about it on the phone. I'm not on no bullshit. I know I keep talkin' about trying to spend time with you but it's not that. I really need to link with you. I don't wanna see nothing bad happen to you," Ant tried to sound sincere.

I couldn't even imagine what the fuck could be going on that would put me in danger because Carter hadn't said nothing. Ant did sound kind of serious. But I couldn't be out here just meeting him in public, Carter knew too many niggas for that shit.

"Do you remember where my cousin vacation house at?" I asked

"Yeah, ain't it like going towards Pittsburgh?" he tried to sound like he really didn't remember.

"Yeah, the address is 890 Sunset Drive. You can meet me there Thursday like around five," I said before hanging up.

I was over everything today. From being pregnant, to this weird ass bitch in the mall, to Ant's bullshit, I was completely over it. I was ready to take my ass home and cuddle under my man. I already decided in my mind that I wouldn't tell Carter anything until I got to the bottom of everything.

***

When I got home, I felt like I was starving. I decided to cook some steak, shrimp, baked potato, and broccoli and cheese. I've been being lazy lately, but I know exactly why I was feeling like that now. While I put dinner on, I decided to clean the house and change the house around. I truly had so much on my mind, and this is what I did to keep my mind at ease. After I finished cooking and cleaning, I was exhausted. I took a hot shower and laid down for a nap.

I didn't mean to sleep the rest of the day away. I was rudely awaken when Carter came in. He had to warm his plate himself, I mean it wouldn't kill him to come in at a decent time. Even though he woke me up, I was happy he was home. I missed him, so I sat up rubbing my eyes.

"Bae, I'm not tryin' to be fat! Den who gon' want me?" I laughed as he shared his food with me.

"Bae, imma always want you. You'll be my butterball bae!" he started cracking up.

"Shut up! That's not even that funny!" I playfully punched him. "You need to come in at a decent time so I can eat my own food and you can eat yours!"

"Bae you still eat my food even when you have your own." He laughed even more.

I glared at him. He had all the jokes in the world. His ass knew I was serious.

"You know what I'm tryin' to say, while you're tryin' to be cute." I smirked.

"Aww bae, you know I be working doe. It's still the beginning of the month. You know my regulars come through at a certain time. Don't act like that!" He kissed my forehead.

I knew I was just being a brat, but he already knew that. He really didn't pay much attention to my whining butt.

***

Thursday came quicker than I thought. I still didn't tell

Carter about the baby or Ant calling or about a weird hoe he most likely used to fuck with coming up to me in the mall. I pulled up at work dressed like I had to work. I told Carter a whole lie about having some extra training, and then having to drive my god sister back to school in PA. He didn't say too much but to check in as usual.

"La'Mea, why are you dressed like your comin' to work?" Melissa asked, calling me back into the examination room.

"Shit, I had to tell Carter something, I still didn't tell him." I confessed.

"Girl what the hell is you waiting for?" she yelled

"Nothin', I just wanna know everything before I just tell him. You already know he gon' have a million questions. I just wanna make sure I can answer every last one of them." I gave her a smart smirk. "I know him, I gotta have all my ducks in a row."

Melissa couldn't argue with that. She didn't really know Carter, just the side confessions here and there. Niggas always had some questions, even though being pregnant was self-explanatory. It really wasn't too many questions that he could ask, other than how far along. I was so excited though once I saw my little tad pole in my stomach, and I heard the heartbeat. My smile was from ear to ear. Melissa smiled too. I was happy she decided to stick around with me. She was cool; I could see us becoming good friends. I kind of felt bad because I didn't even tell my two best friends. Jakirra and DeAsia were going to kill me once they found out. I decided to grab them and make them ride with me out to meet Ant. I definitely didn't want to go by myself no way.

I picked them up after I left the doctor. They got in the car hyped too. I told them about meeting Ant, and they went crazy.

"Carter is going to kill you," DeAsia declared. "Imma let them know at the funeral I tried to warn yo ass!"

"She hardheaded as fuck and you know that!" Jakirra added. "She wants us to be best friendless. Ain't nobody on your shit whatsoever! Den she fuck with a nigga that don't let too much get past him. He's well known, bitch you just like playing with fire!"

"Ya'll are exaggerating about nothing. Carter isn't gonna find out. We're going out to Coco's vacation house. Like how is he gon' find out? And ya'll will be in the car and ya'll will allow us to be in there for no more than twenty minutes before one of ya'll will call and we're out. Quick, sweet, and simple." I had it all figured out. "Plus, I need to make it back to tell my man that I'm pregnant!"

"WHAT?" they both yelled.

"Bitch since when? How long have you known!" Jakirra yelled again.

"I just found out today, I'm 11 weeks." I smiled.

"Omg so why are we meeting Ant again? Because I would be tryin' to go see my man to tell him the news!" DeAsia interrupted.

"Ant claimed some crazy shit about to go down and I need to know what it is. I can't have nothing happen to me or my family," I explained.

"Oh, and let me guess, ya'll couldn't discuss it over the phone?" DeAsia rolled her eyes. "Top secret huh?"

"Bitch, not top secret, but he claims he couldn't say it over the phone. Ya'll know he just got out the feds, you never know, he probably felt like someone could have been listening." I tried to give him the benefit of a doubt.

They both continued their bullshit until we got to the house. Ant's car was pulled all the way in the back and he was standing outside smoking a blunt. I ran the plan down to them again and walked into the house. Ant put his blunt out and followed behind me moments later.

"What's up, Ant?" I shook my head once he walked in smiling from ear to ear.

"Man, don't act like that. You used to love me. Now a nigga can't even get a time of day," he said, now leaning on the counter.

"Look, Ant, you know the situation. I have a nigga, not no I'm just fucking someone like we were. Shit, I respect my man, like I should, and I just refuse to be on some disloyal shit," I explained. "So, like I said what's so important, and top secret that you couldn't discuss on the phone?"

"I'm so glad you mentioned disloyalty. How can you be loyal to a nigga that's not loyal to you doe? That's all I'm tryin' to understand," Ant replied. "I mean, I understand you gotta nigga and you clearly love him, but how well do you really know this nigga?"

I knew Ant was trying to just get under my skin. I wasn't down for him disrespecting my man whatsoever. I really hope this wasn't what we came all this way out here to talk about.

"Ant, I'm tryin' to understand why the fuck does this concern you though? Do you know him? No! So, Imma ask you again, what's so important and top secret that you couldn't talk to me over the phone." I was annoyed.

"Look man, I'm tryin' to let you know you don't know your nigga like you think you do!" Ant cleared his throat. "Shit, he's fucking another bitch on the side, so what you think about that."

"You are so sad, you gotta come better den that, Ant," I was amused. "You think Imma be like omg he fucking another bitch and start fucking you? Cut the shit! This was a complete waste of time. I don't even know why I came. This was a mistake."

I started walking towards the door, I couldn't believe I even wasted my gas to come out here for nothing. He had me fucked up. I wasn't even about to entertain his bullshit.

"La'Mea, he's about to meet his other bitch right now at the Double Tree in room 326. She's working with me. I used you, bitch. You're my alibi when my niggas run in there and kill his ass and take him for everything he got." He burst out laughing.

I felt my whole body go numb. What the fuck was he talking about? I turned around and looked at him in disbelief.

"What?" I wanted him to repeat himself.

"You heard me. The bitch he fucking is putting down the play right now," he laughed. "I guess you don't know your nigga after all."

"Ant, you're full of shit." I put my purse down on the couch, I was about to let him have it. "You will do and say anything. I will never fuck with you though. I have a future with him. You can't do for me what he does. Sorry! Leave me and my family alone. Don't call me anymore or nothing. I have to focus on my baby coming soon."

Ant's facial expression changed drastically. He was pissed. If he was white, he would have been red as a beet.

"You're pregnant by this nigga," Ant said, pulling out his phone.

"Yes, we're going to have a family so you and that bitch, whoever she is, can go choke on one!" I smirked.

"Well, it looks like yo baby is gon' need a daddy, baby girl because he's good as dead!" Ant said, placing his phone back in his pocket smiling.

A part of me just regretted telling him that. I didn't know if it was the fact he was on his phone that scared me, but I just had a bad feeling all of a sudden. I ran over to my purse. Right when I picked up my purse, Ant snatched it away and threw it on the other couch.

"What you think your doin'? You think your about to call and warn that nigga. Bitch sit down. We gon' wait for the call," Ant said, forcing me to the couch. "I had big plans for us. This coulda worked, Mea. We could have been a family, but no."

"Ant, let me go now!" I yelled hoping my best friends would hear me.

"Shut the fuck up," Ant said, grabbing my mouth.

I snatched away from him and ran back towards my phone. It seemed as if I was running in slow motion because this nigga was on my ass. He snatched me again so quickly. I had remembered Coco kept so many hunting knives all over the house just in case. I reached in the couch and pulled out a small hunting knife, and pointed it directly at him.

"Ant, please, just let me go," I cried out. "Just leave or let me leave. I don't care what ya'll have going on. I just wanna go."

He looked at me in disbelief. I don't know what was running through his mind, but I just wanted him away from me. He came towards me again and I stabbed him. It seemed like it did nothing because he bear hugged me. I could feel the tears falling from my eyes as I stabbed him four more times. He fell to the ground; blood poured out. I had blood all over me.

"Oh my God," I yelled with blood covering my hands.

What the hell just happened? Why did he charge at me like that? I looked down at the blood spreading on the floor. It was everywhere? I shouldn't have never came! How was I going to explain this shit. Carter was going to kill me. I ran over to my coat and searched for my phone. Fumbling through my call long, I called Jakirra.

"Damn, I hope you're not fucking that nigga?" Jakirra chuckled as she answered the phone.

"I think he's dead!" I cried out. "Please come in here. Best, I think I killed him."

Jakirra never responded. Moments later, her and DeAsia was standing in the doorway in disbelief. I could tell by the looks on their faces they had no idea what the fuck to do.

"La'Mea what the hell happened?" Jakirra yelled.

"What have you done?" DeAsia asked, getting closer to the body to see if he was really dead. "Did you at least check and see if he had a chance of living? I mean is he really dead?"

They both looked at me awaiting an answer. I still said nothing. I looked over at the body and looked down to the floor. I just stood there in silence. All this felt like a bad dream. I never meant for none of this to happen. All I wanted to do is protect the people I loved.

"DeAsia, check and make sure he's dead!" Jakirra ordered.

DeAsia eyes got big as hell. She looked at the body twice then back at Jakirra. She just knew she misheard what Jakirra just asked her to do.

"Umm, bitch, I didn't kill him. I'm definitely ain't about to touch him. Lil crazy better get over here and check and see if he's dead." She rolled her eyes and backed up. "Ya'll got me fucked up. I'm going to jail with ya'll hoes today. I'm not!"

Jakirra completely tuned her out. She walked over and leaned close to examine his body. She looked over at me again.

"Best, I think he's really dead!" she said calmly. "LA'MEA!"

She kept yelling my name. In my head I wanted to tell her what happened, but I was numb; I didn't move, and I didn't speak. I just stood there in complete silence.

"Jakirra, call somebody, the police, somebody!" DeAsia called out. "Omg what did you do, Mea? I knew we shouldn't have come!"

"DeAsia, shut the fuck real quick let me think!" Jakirra yelled at her. "La'Mea, who all knew ya'll was meeting here?"

I still didn't say anything, I walked over to the couch and sat down, never taking my eyes off Ant's body! I didn't mean to kill him; this wasn't supposed to happen! Jakirra pulled out her phone and started to call someone.

"Hello," Jakirra said frantic now.

"What wrong, baby?" Ced asked once he caught the panic in her voice.

"I need you to come to where I am right now. It's an emergency," Jakirra said. "Like now Ced."

I never moved even when she said his name.

"What going on, Jakirra?" Ced sounded concerned. "Where are you? Is someone there with you? If they are just say I love you or something like that."

"No, it's not that. Baby, please just come here," Jakirra pleaded. "I can't tell you over the phone."

"I got Cartier and Carter with me. I need you to send me the address where you at!" He finally gave up trying to make her tell him what was going on.

"DeAsia, go look at the address for me!" Jakirra ordered before she noticed a piece of mail sitting on the table. "Never mind, baby the address is 890 Sunset Drive. Please hurry."

Jakirra hung up and sat on the couch next to me. She said nothing; she wrapped her arms around me and just held me. DeAsia was walking back and forth on the floor so much I thought she was going to eventually fall through.

Ant

I was happy as fuck Monea was really considering helping me bring this nigga down. I knew we both had our reasons, but shit I could care less. I was so happy when Monea called out the blue saying that she would go through with the plans; I didn't know what changed her mind, but I wasn't trying to find out either. I told her after everything went down, we could go to Miami for a little while. We were going to definitely need a break because shit was going to get crazy. Shit was really looking gravy for me once I convinced La'Mea to meet me out at her people's house. Shit couldn't have lined up better. I didn't even plan to take that kind of trip, but I knew couldn't shit get traced back to me.

***

I pulled up to King's house and everybody was standing in the yard talking shit. It felt good to be free. I missed being out here with these niggas man, and to make shit better I was about to back in the game like I never left. I couldn't complain about shit. When I walked up, I dapped everybody up, and passed the blunt to my brother.

"Ya'll niggas always smoking! Ya'll need to leave that shit alone!" Shawn said, shaking his head. "What's the move with that one shit?"

"Shit, everything in line. I came over here to see how ya'll wanted to do this." I said, sitting on the porch.

"So, you tell us the basics," King said.

"Well, Carter's side bitch and my bitch, Monea, will meet Carter at the hotel for their normal one two, and den somewhere in between, that's when ya'll come in. Shit, I told her that he wouldn't get hurt, but this shit won't work unless he's dead." I said, getting right to the point.

"And you sure this little hoe ain't going to change up on you?" King asked concerned.

"Man, she called me and told me it's a go. I mean, I don't think she would change up. That nigga Carter playin' her too," I explained.

"Shit, all you gotta tell us is the time and the place, and you know we got it from there," Dezmond replied, loading one of his guns.

I was satisfied with their responses. I knew they were ready for a come up. Business wasn't the same since Jeez and them started getting locked up. Shit had gotten really fucked up, and our goal was to get everybody back eating.

***

I had a lot to do Thursday; I had to first meet with Monea to make sure her head was in the right place. I never really asked her the reason why she changed her mind; I needed her not to let her emotions get in the way because this was a job. If she could pull this off with a nigga she cared about, I had big plans for her in the future because I know baby girl is a savage.

When I walked in the hotel, she was laying across the bed with nothing but her pants on. I smiled, I had time to slide in it before I had to meet La'Mea.

"Hey, love." I playfully smacked her ass.

"Hey, daddy." She rolled over to give me a pussy shot.

"You ready for this shit?" I asked laying down with her. "Are you scared?"

"Nah baby, I'm ready. We going to get this money and live. But most of all I'm ready for Miami. I need a vacation!" she said, rubbing my chest. "I wanna be able to walk on the sandy beach and sip on fly ass tropical drinks.

She laid across the bed ready to take this dick. We didn't have to waste any time. I slowly entered her, and she couldn't help but tense up.

"You cool, love? You want me to stop?" I asked not used to that.

She moaned softly. "No, keep going."

She couldn't refrain from moaning loud and gripping the sheets. Flipping her over, and placing her legs on my shoulders, I began stroking every corner she had. I watched her bite her lip; I knew she about ready to cum.

"Oh my God. I'm cumin', ooohhh!" she screamed as I kept pumping, now going even faster. "Oh my God."

The moans came back to back. Her pussy was wet as fuck. Laying her on her side, I kept stroking until I finally came too.

"Damn, baby, that pussy was good as fuck," I said, kissing her cheek.

"I missed you." She pouted playfully.

"Everything is going to be good. After we hit this lick, we going to be right. I promise," I assured her.

It kind of felt good being around Monea, I didn't know it could feel like this. It made me second guess wanting La'Mea's ass back. I placed a bag of money under the sink, and headed to meet La'Mea.

***

I couldn't help but admire how pretty La'Mea looked when she got out the car. I noticed her friends in the car, but they didn't follow us in the house. This shit was even better, her nosey ass friends could be a witness to seeing me here with Mea. Nobody could have ever told me this conversation would go left. From the moment she told me she was pregnant by this nigga, I completely lost my mind. I wanted that nigga dead. I was supposed to be her baby's father. I was supposed to be the one she started a family with. Not him. He was playing on her with Monea. While she was talking her shit, I shot Dezmond a text:

Kill that nigga. Everything is a go. Make sure ya'll don't hurt Monea though!

I was pissed off. I couldn't believe the shit she was just saying to me. This used to be my bitch. She used to love me, but now she is treating me like a nigga don't mean shit. I couldn't take that shit. I couldn't even put my head around it. I felt my phone vibrate.

Bet. We got this!

I was satisfied with his response. I placed my phone back in the couch and decided to turn up on this bitch now. Her precious relationship would be no more, that perfect family she was hoping for would just be a thought. After forcing her to the couch, she tried to run for her purse to warn this weak ass nigga. I wasn't planning to hurt her bad, I didn't give a fuck about her allegations of being pregnant. Then she pulled a knife out. I laughed to myself, she wasn't about that life. It didn't even have to result to this. All this bitch had to do was be patient, and wait until this job was done. I never thought this bitch would stab me.

After the first time she stabbed me, I was still in shock. I bear hugged her to bring her down, and she stabbed me four more times. All I could think about were my babies. This wasn't a part of my plan. She allowed my body to fall to the floor. The girl that once loved me, just stabbed me, and now she was watching me die. She just stood there, and never said a word. Who would have thought this would be my destiny.

Carter

I swear even though everything was going good at home with La'Mea, I missed Monea. She did something for me. It was like they both put my life at an equal balance. So, when she hit me up the other day about having a night at the hotel, I really couldn't pass it up.

"So, what's up baby," I said when she answered

"Are you still down for our perfect night?" Monea asked sounding sexy.

"Of course, I am. I gotta make a couple moves with my brothers den Imma be der," I assured her.

"Well don't take too long, Double Tree downtown, room 326. Your key will be waiting at the desk for you."

"Okay love, I will see you in a few," I said before hanging up.

***

I swear sometimes the drug business can get annoying. Niggas just always feel like because we gotta the product and or the bread, it shouldn't be a problem for us to take losses or look out. I was super pissed because this weird ass nigga sold us a bad pack and was playing crazy. That's just something my brothers and I didn't play about. When we pulled up at the spot this nigga looked like he seen a ghost.

"Look at the money boys, what do I owe this visit," Mario said like he didn't know.

"Man, cut the shit. That pack was bullshit. We been hittin' yo ass up and you been dodging us." Ced got right to the chase.

"Man, I ain't have nothing to do with that, I got it from my connect and gave it right to you. No fishy or funny shit." Mario tried to sound convincing.

We weren't trying to hear that shit, something had to be

done. We weren't about to take no big ass loss like that. It was unheard of in my book.

"How can I make this right, we do too much business to create bad blood between us," Mario tried to compromise.

"Shit, only thing I can see happening is we get our money back or some more shit," Cartier suggested.

"Man, ya'll know I can't just do either one." Mario froze up.

"Look, this shit can get ugly. We can make sure that you don't sell shit else in these streets my nigga! Niggas will get to droppin' like flies, now do you wanna take your chance with that?" I was over the bullshit.

"No need for that doe, Carter. We are better than that. This is business doe."

"I don't give a fuck about the shit you're talking about. This is the offer; you give half back in drugs and half of our money back and we can call it even. That's all I'm offering and then I'm going to start making shit happen." I was pissed off.

"Okay, Okay, I think we can make that happen." Mario was relieved.

The shit went smoother than I expected. I really wanted to shoot some shit up and make good on my word. As a man, my word was bond. I assured him, next time, shit wouldn't come this easy. Next time niggas was going to play for trying to fuck over us. Mario assured us we could finish business tomorrow; he claims he didn't have the stuff there and needed to get the money together.

On our way back home, I looked at my brother and couldn't help but to feel good. We had come a long way from living and hustling in the projects to here. The come up was great but to get out the game for good and live life was our real purpose.

"Brah, you ready for this shit," Ced said turning down the music.

"Shit, I'm ready to just get this money for real," I replied.

"Just to get out the game and really live like royalty is what I want," Cartier added. "Shit we gon' be good. I'm ready."

"Shit we going to be good, patience is key." I shrugged.

The ride home was great. We didn't have to kill nor hurt nobody and that was always a plus. I turned up the music again and tried to enjoy life.

***

We were just about home when Ced's phone started ringing. He turned down the music, and smiled.

"My lil freak," he laughed as he answered the phone.

I tuned his ass out, I was just trying to get back so I could see my bitch. Cartier had dozed off in the back, so I didn't have nobody to talk shit to, so I looked out the window at the open road ahead.

"Brah," Ced broke my train of thought.

"What's up?" I looked over at him and instantly knew something was wrong.

"You gotta go back right this minute because Jakirra just called panicking and she's like three exits from here," Ced explained.

"Go head, brah, I'm meeting Monea, but I told her I would be a minute." I sat back and was ready to just go for the ride. "Handle your business."

***

When we pulled up, the first thing I noticed was La'Mea car parked at the end of the driveway. I sat up and looked again.

"La'Mea with her?" I looked confused.

"I don't know, I heard her say DeAsia's name. I never heard said Mea name. Maybe they used her car," Ced suggested.

I tapped Cartier and we all got out the car. I didn't know what the hell we were about to walk into, but we went to the trunk and loaded up just in case. Nobody could have prepared us for what we were about to walk into. The nigga, Ant, was lying in a puddle of blood, La'Mea was covered in blood, DeAsia was pacing the floor, and Jakirra was standing in the kitchen with a drink in her hand completely disturbed.

"What the fuck happen in here?" Ced asked, breaking the silence. Nobody spoke up at first. I looked around at all their blank looks.

"Ask your sister in law, she's the real thug in this bitch!" DeAsia rolled her eyes. "She's the blame for all this shit!"

All eyes turned to La'Mea. I was waiting on her to speak up. She still sat there looking at the body lying on the floor. I knew I was about to spazz. What the fuck was this bitch doing with this nigga anyway.

"It was an accident, this shit just got outta hand too quick," Jakirra finally spoke up trying to make something sound good.

"What the fuck you mean? Why the fuck are ya'll all the way out here with this nigga by ya'll self. La'Mea you told me you were picking yo people up from PA?" I began to get angrier.

"We were going to do that, but they ended up changing they mind and got a ride with someone else and called at the last..." Jakirra continued.

"That's a fucking lie, Ant called La'Mea and told her that he needed to talk to her, he said they couldn't talk over the phone so killa Mea told him to meet her here! Stop lyin,' Jakirra!" DeAsia yelled. "I'm not going to jail for you bitch, I'm too cute to be someone's bitch!"

Jakirra looked as she wanted to rip DeAsia's whole head off. She took another sip of her drink but said nothing. DeAsia swallowed hard after looking at Jakirra. I just knew it was going to be another murder.

"Bae don't lie, what the hell is really going on?" Ced turned to Jakirra.

She shook her head and simply shrugged her shoulders. "Bae, I don't know. La'Mea still haven't told us. We got the call to come in here. We really were sitting in the car."

I was really pissed off. What type of bullshit was this bitch trying to pull. The expression on my brother's face wasn't ten times as bad as mine was. I felt fucking embarrassed. This bitch still was acting like a fucking mute, like she was just oblivious to what the fuck was going on. This shit was fishy as fuck.

"La'Mea?" I said, walking towards her. "What the fuck happened?"

She still didn't open her mouth. I wanted to punch her; this bitch knew she heard me. I never disrespected her, she knew that, but she was really testing me. Out of nowhere she got up and walked over to Jakirra and stood against the stove like I wasn't even talking to her.

"La'Mea don't do that, you hear me talking to you." I started walking over towards her. "Why the fuck was you in here with this nigga alone? What the fuck did he have to talk about that was so important he couldn't tell you over the phone? And why the fuck did he even have your fuckin' number."

Before I knew it, I wrapped my hands around her neck. I felt like she was trying to play me like a fuck nigga by not answering me. I wasn't feeling that bullshit whatsoever. This was the first time she had spoken since I walked in the door. I was so zoned out; I didn't hear shit though.

"Let her go, brah!" Ced said, finally pulling me off of her. "You can deal with her later; we need to get this shit cleaned up and out the way asap!"

"Yeah, brah, this shit can get ugly if someone walk in and this body just laying here," Cartier reminded us.

"Is someone coming back here tonight?" Ced looked over to Mea.

She shook her head no. Ced looked back at me and just shook his head.

"I gotta go. I didn't kill nobody, I'm not about to be a part of this bullshit at all," DeAsia said, walking towards the door.

"How the fuck are you getting home. Bitch we all rode together!" Jakirra yelled.

"Look, DeAsia yo ass been here, whatever gotta be done bitch yo ass going to help too! Now shut the fuck up and allow us to think of something because clearly you bitches couldn't!" Cartier said, stepping in front of the door. "Because if ya'll asses did we wouldn't even be here, let alone know about this fuck shit!"

"I didn't do shit! I didn't kill anybody so you're not fucking talking to me! I don't know who you're talking to, but I'm not involved. Whatever needs to be done Killa Mea better fucking do it," she shot back. "I keep telling ya'll I'M NOT GOING TO JAIL FOR

NOBODY!"

"DeAsia shut the fuck up man, like I said yo ass got in the car and was down for the ride so yo ass going to ride this shit out!" Cartier pushed her away from the door. "Sit the fuck down somewhere and shut the fuck up!"

DeAsia could tell Cartier wasn't playing. Her ass walked over the couch and sat down. Everybody was on edge. I knew for certain nobody was going to jail, we just needed a plan, and a good one at that. I took myself on a tour of the house. I walked in the basement and I had the perfect idea. I ran back upstairs to the awkward silence.

"We're gonna burn everything that has been exposed to the blood, including the body. This place has to be cleaned from top to bottom, nobody can ever know any of us was here." I looked around at everyone. "Yo ass over there acting like a fuckin' mute, yo ass gon' help with yo disloyal ass!"

I must have hit a nerve because La'Mea finally spoke up.

"Disloyal? You got yo fuckin' nerve! Bitch I only came here because Ant made me think the feds was on you. I came here only to find out he was planning on robbing yo dumb ass today when you were supposed to be meeting your side bitch at the Double Tree in room 326!" she yelled. "I only stabbed him because he tried to stop me from calling and telling you. So, if anybody disloyal it's yo dumb ass! Fucking with these snake ass hoes."

"You sound dumb, ain't nobody meeting nobody at no fucking hotel, that nigga lied to you!" I lied.

"Carter, all I wanted was a family! I was just meeting him so he could tell me whatever he needed to tell so I could come home and tell my man that I was pregnant!" I busted out in tears. "This wasn't supposed to happen!"

"Who are you pregnant by?" I asked.

Although, I already knew about the pregnancy, I just felt like she should have been told me. What the fuck was she waiting so long for?

"Don't do that, Carter." She rolled her eyes. "I ain't been fucking nobody but you!"

"Nah, you been fuckin' me and Ant, right?" I said sarcastically.

I could see her getting mad; she got up and charged towards me. Every time she swung, she missed. She was pissed off. I finally mugged her to the couch. I didn't have time to be fighting with her. I pushed her away and headed over to the bathroom to get the towels. I didn't have time for her shit. We had to get rid of this body. Shit I had so many unanswered questions. And how the fuck did she know about me meeting Monea and the room number? Was that a lucky guess or did she really know?

***

Cartier, Ced, and I carried the body downstairs, the girls followed with the bloody towels and rags. I couldn't believe this shit. This wasn't the first time having to clean a mess up, and I knew for sure it wasn't going to be our last. I just didn't think it would be my bitch killing someone. As much as she stressed that it was an accident, a part of me felt like if Jakirra never called Ced, and I wasn't in the car, I would have never known nothing about none of this.

"Open the door to the furnace," I ordered.

DeAsia walked over and opened the square opening. They all took a final look at the body, everybody except La'Mea, she was looking down at the blood on her clothes and shoes. After we stuffed the body in the furnace, I looked back at La'Mea.

"Is there some extra clothes here?" I asked her.

"I'm pretty sure it is somewhere upstairs. Why?" she uttered.

"Jakirra run upstairs and look for some clothes." I reopened the furnace. "Take yo shit off, that shit gotta go!"

La'Mea slowly took off her clothes, Jakirra quickly returned with a Pink Jogging suit and some flip flops. She grabbed the clothes and walked over to the bathroom and closed the door. Everybody headed back upstairs to make sure everything was good. I stayed behind to wait for Mea.

"So, did you fuck that nigga?" I asked soon as the bathroom door opened.

La'Mea rolled her eyes.

"No, I told you, I came to meet him because he said we couldn't talk over the phone. When I got in here shit just went left so fast. I was tryin' to leave."

"Yo ass never shoulda came. You shoulda told me La'Mea. This nigga was calling you and shit!" I yelled. "How long have ya'll been having these secret conversations? Why you questioning if I talked to the nigga! Is that the real reason you ain't want me to do business with him because yo ass was trying to fuck back with him?"

"No, he wasn't. That was the first time I seen him since the day at Walmart," she stated. "And I still stand behind you not working with him because I knew he had other plans too."

"Hold the fuck up, you seen this nigga at Walmart?" I asked confused. "You just got all the secrets huh?"

"Yeah, I didn't say nothing because it was so innocent!" she yelled. "Carter you're all down my back, you were meeting this hoe at Double Tree!"

"I don't know what the fuck you're talking about. That's that bullshit yo weak ass little boyfriend lied and told yo dumb ass. He wanted to fuck you that's all, dummy," I said sarcastically.

"Nah that nigga wasn't lying, Carter! They were playing on robbing yo dumb ass little do you know!" She got mad again and acted as if she was going to run up again.

"So why you ain't been tell you that you were pregnant? Because you been knew! Is it because it wasn't mine?" I changed the subject. "Is that why you were meeting this nigga to tell him ya'll slipped up?"

"What? Carter, you sound dumb as fuck! I didn't do shit but meet this nigga so we could talk. I wasn't fucking him! He got mad because I told him that we were about to have a family. That's why he got so mad, I tried to leave, and he wouldn't let me. I didn't mean to kill him; I swear I didn't!" She finally broke down. "I never cheated on you."

A part of me wanted to comfort her. I wanted to believe her, my head was so fucked up, I didn't know what to think. I watched her slide to the floor and bury her face in her lap. I pulled out my phone and looked at the time. Monea hadn't called or nothing, and it was getting late. I walked over and grabbed her arm and made her come upstairs.

***

"Everything is good, but what are we going to do with this nigga's car?" Cartier asked as I walked through the door. "That bitch definitely can't stay here after we leave!"

I never even seen the car. I didn't even think about how this nigga got here.

"Shit, we gotta meet the plug tomorrow right?" Ced confirmed.

"Yeah, at like twelve. What does that have to do with it?" I was trying to see what he was getting at.

"Shit, we all stay here tonight, I drive my car, and one of ya'll drive that nigga's car. We can dump it somewhere," Ced suggested. "That's the only thing we can do. Nothing can trace him back here. Nobody can trace any of us for being here."

I thought for a moment and that didn't sound like a bad idea. That nigga did need to find a new plug, shit could have went bad during the buy. I didn't have any objections to the idea, I already chalked me seeing Monea. I sat on the couch and nodded my head.

"I'm not staying here. I refuse to stay where someone was killed at. His body is downstairs burning as we speak. Oh, hell nah!" DeAsia shouted. "Ya'll got me fucked up. La'Mea take me home now!"

"Ain't nobody going no fucking where. You heard what my brother said. When we leave out tomorrow then yo ass can go home, unless yo ass wanna walk!" Cartier blasted.

"Cartier, stop talking to me, please!" she rolled her eyes and yelled. "I just can't stay here."

"Welp, you are now so shut up," Jakirra added. "You're not helping this situation. We will leave first thing in the morning. All your bullshit that you're going through, cut it out. It's not always about DeAsia."

“Shit, it’s about La’Mea though! She made this mess and now we all are suckered into this bullshit,” DeAsia said, throwing shots.

“Bitch please, ain’t nobody said that shit either but you’re over there extra dramatic like a big ass baby and shit. We’re staying til' the morning that’s that. Now shut up and sit the fuck down somewhere damn,” Jakirra said, finally fed up with DeAsia’s shit.
I sat back and still didn’t say nothing. I watched La’Mea, who was sitting next to me, playing with her string on the jogging suit. Something just wasn’t sitting right with me. Did she go through my phone? Did he really know Monea? I studied her face. It was so blank; I couldn’t even imagine what was going through her mind.

La'Mea

I couldn't believe this nigga tried to flip this shit on me. I wanted to kill him; I knew that the shit Ant told me wasn't a lie. I knew it had some truth, especially when I brought it up, this nigga's whole demeanor changed. I never cheated on him, but Carter knew that. I felt so fucked up though. I knew I put all of them in this fucked up position. DeAsia was completely losing her fucking mind, Cartier and Ced wasn't on this shit but because I was his brother's girl, they didn't have a choice, and Jakirra she was just quiet for real. I knew sorry just wasn't good enough. I definitely felt DeAsia about staying here, I knew I wasn't going to get no sleep. I was already feeling uncomfortable sitting across from the blood-stained floor. I watched them clean up the rest of the mess and take it downstairs to be burned.

"Mea, you need to eat. Is it okay that we cook some food?" Jakirra said, finally breaking the moment of silence.

I nodded. I never looked up. I continued to fidget with my clothes. I knew all eyes was on me. I couldn't deal. I got up and ran to the bathroom; I felt so sick. Carter and Jakirra was right on my heels.

"Are you okay, best?" Jakirra asked, grabbing my hair as I threw up.

"Bae, are you cool?" Carter looked concerned.

"Yeah, I'm good," I said, grabbing the tissue and wiping my mouth.

"I'm about to cook something, just lay down and relax, best," Jakirra ordered.

I looked at both of them and walked back into the living room and laid on the couch.

***

Jakirra cooked a nice dinner, we all ate and sat around trying to collect our thoughts about this situation. I finally got up and grabbed covers and pillows for everyone. I really was just ready for this night to be over. I wanted to go home.

"So Mea, did you find out how far along you are?" DeAsia tried to spark a conversation.

"Eleven weeks," I mumbled.

"Are you excited?" she continued.

I looked over at Carter who was focused on whatever was going on with his phone on the opposite end of the couch. I was looking for a smile that he was happy about the baby, but I knew that he wasn't on it right now.

"Yes, I really am, regardless of the bullshit that has happened," I admitted.

"I hope you have a girl. I always wanted to see all my friends with girls first, just so ya'll can dress alike and shit like that!" She smiled. "I'm happy for you."

"Thanks, best!" I tried to smile.

"Me too," Jakirra added. "Now you can have someone to drive you crazy."

I wanted to ask Carter was he excited but shit he thought I was fucking Ant, and if he would have said some crazy shit again, I was going to beat the fuck out of him. Well at least try anyway because I wasn't on his shit whatsoever. I looked around at everybody. Jakirra and Ced was now cuddled up on the far side of the room. DeAsia and Cartier was on the sectional on opposite ends, just like me and Carter. I turned on the tv and kicked at Carter.

"What?" he finally looked up from his phone.

"Come here," I said softly. "Please."

At first he didn't move, I knew he was pissed off at me, just like I was with him. I didn't care what he said, I knew if all this didn't happen his ass would have come up with an excuse why he wasn't coming home and was going to be at that hotel. He slowly moved to my end of the couch.

"What Mea?"

"Look, I understand you're pissed off at me, but I swear I only came here because I thought he was trying to warn me about something serious. When I found out his real intentions, I was trying to leave. I wasn't on any bullshit," I tried to explain. "He was planning on using me as his alibi when all the bullshit went down. I was never planning to kill him, but I had no choice."

Carter didn't say nothing at first, but when he looked at me, he knew I wasn't lying. I didn't have a reason to. I had been nothing but a hundred and solid since day one. Carter was my heart and at the moment I felt I had to do what I had to do. I felt like I was protecting my family.

"I'm sorry," he said rubbing my thighs. "I was planning on meeting the crazy bitch at the hotel, but she ain't mean shit doe. She was just something to do from time to time when we weren't getting along. She called me, and said she wanted to see me, and I hadn't seen her in a minute and that's all it was. She used to take rides with me, on drops and shit like that. The nigga Ant must have got to her."

I couldn't believe my ears. Tears rolled down my face, I didn't even wanna look around and see who all caught hold of our conversation. I wanted to fight him. I wanted to scream and tell him to go to hell.

"Wow?!" I was stuck, that was some honesty for my ass.

I stood up and walked into the kitchen. I didn't even want to talk to him. It was true the grass wasn't always greener on the other side. I thought Jeez took me through some shit, this situation ain't have shit on his bullshit. We didn't speak for the rest of the night; I think that was the best decision that we ever could have made.

***

When I woke up, the boys were already gone, Ant's rental was gone, and the girls were standing in front of the picture glass window talking amongst themselves. I knew I couldn't take shit back all this was my fault. Well now I can put a little blame on Carter's dumb ass because if he was never fucking that scandalous ass bitch, Ant would have never had a way in. He gave him that. I was super pissed about that.

"Are ya'll ready to go?" I asked, standing up stretching.

"We waiting on you, baby." Jakirra quickly turned around.

"Let me clean this little bit of shit up and check on downstairs and then we can go."

"And never ever come back either," DeAsia added.

I couldn't help to agree with her. This wasn't going to be a first pick to vacation at to getaway no more. This place would forever hunt me. This was going to be a secret they all took to the grave.

It had been a few days since we got back home, I was laying on couch when it sounded as if the police were banging on my front door. I jumped up so fast and ran to the door to see.

"Why the hell are you banging on the door like that?" I yelled in Jakirra's face as I opened the door.

"Bitch we have a problem!" she stormed in. Before I could shut the door, Cartier was pulling up to.

"Aye, Carter sent me over here to get something," he said, hopping out the car.

He headed upstairs and we went into the kitchen so he couldn't hear us.

"What's wrong?" I immediately asked.

"Girl, DeAsia is trippin', she talking about she can't sleep at night, she talking about telling on you and on us. Shit we covered it up. I tried to talk to her, but she won't listen to me." Jakirra was panicking.

This was all I needed was for her to be having guilty thoughts now. We didn't have time for this shit. I wasn't trying to go to jail, shit especially being pregnant. I never heard Cartier leave, but when I ran upstairs to grab my phone he was nowhere to be found. Jakirra met me at the bottom of the stairs.

"What the plan?" she asked.

"I'm about to call her and tell her we going to come over so we can talk. She just needs to be assured that this shit is going to work out," I replied dialing her number.

"What's up, best?" she answered on the first ring.

"What you doing today?"

"Shit, just chillin' around the house. I need to get some rest; I haven't been sleeping really good," she explained.

"Well, Jakirra and I might stop by a little later just to have a glass of wine and talk, that probably will help you sleep," I suggested.

"Cool, just come through, I will be here," she said before hanging up.

I turned and looked at Jakirra and shook my head. DeAsia didn't even sound like herself. She sounded as if she was disturbed.

"Damn so what think?" Jakirra uttered.

"We just need to talk to her. Do you think she told someone already?"

"Nah." Jakirra shook her head and looked at the floor.

I found that odd. What the fuck did Jakirra know that I didn't. I didn't even wanna ask just in the fear that this shit was way worse than she wanted me to know. I couldn't be stressing, that shit was bad for the baby.

***

When we pulled up to DeAsia's house, I tried to get all the things I wanted to say together. I needed her to hold it together. We were standing at her door for at least ten minutes, we called, and ran the doorbell and got no answer. She knew we were coming, why wasn't she answering. To make matters worse I had to pee.

"Let's go around the back, she gotta spare key under the grill." Jakirra started walking to the back.

I rolled my eyes. I didn't have time to be trying to break into nobody's house. If she didn't want to answer than fine, I wasn't about to be trying to kiss her ass because sometimes that's what this bitch wanted. She wanted this shit to be about her. A part of me knew for a fact she wasn't going to tell; she knew that these niggas would kill her without a second thought, she played a role in the clean-up process. She was just as guilty as I was.

"Come on, fat girl," Jakirra said once I made it through her maze in the back.

"Shit is a maze. I hate coming to her back door and I have to pee," I complained.

"It's open, come on," she said, turning the door and walking right in.

We walked through and it was so quiet. Her car was in the front so she could have been sleep. I followed Jakirra upstairs and we heard a loud thump. DeAsia's room was a complete mess like she was fighting with someone. I paused as I noticed her bathroom to her bedroom was slightly cracked. I couldn't help but hear the splash noises either. Jakirra and I couldn't believe our eyes.

"NO!" Jakirra yelled, scaring Cartier.

He quickly jumped up covered in water, and stepped back.

"What have you done!" Jakirra ran over and tried to pull DeAsia out the water. "Cartier what did you do?"

I felt like it was déjà vu. We just were starting in the predicament leaving us to cover up my fuck up and now here we were again. Jakirra kept screaming and crying as she let DeAsia limped body fall back into the water. Silent tears rolled down my face. My best friend's limp body was soaking wet. My eyes met Cartier's. I knew then that he heard us earlier. I never noticed Jakirra run past me and Cartier right on her ass. He grabbed her right before she hit the stairs.

"Look at me, Jakirra! Look at me!" Cartier snatched her hair and began to shake her. "It had to be done. She was already planning on talking to the police. She told me that she couldn't live like that, we can't afford to take that chance. I'm not going to jail for nobody! Not you, you, or that bitch in there!"

When he looked at me, I knew he wasn't just playing. I never seen Cartier like this. I didn't know what to think. He still had Jakirra gripped tightly around the neck. I couldn't lose both of my best friends.

"Just let me call Carter, he will know what to do," I suggested, pulling my phone out.

"No! Fuck no! We will handle this. Ya'll will call the police, tell them ya'll showed up to your friend because ya'll had plans, when ya'll got here, she wasn't answering, so ya'll used to spare key in the back, and found her."

"Cartier," Jakirra yelled.

"Ya'll gon' do this or shit ya'll can end up just like her!" he said harshly.

What choice did we really have. All this was getting out of hand. I couldn't believe this nigga but at the same time I knew a lot of this shit was my fault. I mean what other choice did I really have at this point? Turn Cartier in? I looked at Jakirra and picked up my phone. I looked back toward the bathroom where DeAsia was still floating in the tub full of water. I dialed 911 and took a deep breath.

"911 what's your emergency," the dispatcher responded.

"OMG," I began to scream hysterically. "MY FRIEND IS DEAD, OMG I JUST FOUND MY BEST FRIEND DEAD IN HER TUB."

Jakirra's eyes got huge. Yes bitch, I'm an actress. I couldn't believe myself. Cartier looked speechless. I could've won an Emmy award off this performance.

"Ma'am, I need you to calm down. Is your friend responsive?" the dispatcher tried to collect as much information between all my fake ass sobbing I was doing.

"NO PLEASE, WHY DEASIA? HOW COULD SHE HAVE DONE THIS TO HERSELF," I cried out again. "PLEASE JUST SEND SOMEONE."

"They're comin', ma'am. Did you try CPR?"

"NO!" I yelled. "I can't touch her like this."

"Okay they are coming," she assured me.

I dropped the phone and look at the both of them. You could hear the sirens from a distance.

"Look, stick to the story, don't fuck up," Cartier said as he walked out the door.

Jakirra slid to the floor and cried, I couldn't help to comfort my friend. All this was my fault in a fucked up way.

***

When the police arrived, it was like a scene from 'True

Crime Mondays.' They were everywhere. I wasn't really trying to talk to these people. Jakirra couldn't hold it together, she just kept crying, and I thought I needed an award. I didn't have shit on this bitch. We both kept the tears flowing. It was so many unanswered questions, and the detectives weren't even letting me up.

"Do you know anybody that wanted to harm DeAsia?" the detective stood in front of us as we still cried on the couch.

We both shook our heads no. Nobody wanted to harm her. I wanted to tell them so fucking bad that Cartier killed my friend because she said she was going to tell about me killing Ant. How did that part of the truth sound. I couldn't take it, I felt sick. I ran over to the garbage can and begin to throw up. I felt like I was about to die; I was hot and now sweating.

"Is everything okay?" the detective questioned.

"She's pregnant, this all just overwhelming." Jakirra chimed in.

Just as Jakirra was walking over to comfort me, her cell phone began to vibrate on the far table. She quickly shifted directions and answered the phone. I knew quickly from her tone that it was Carter. I walked over to DeAsia's kitchen and grabbed paper towel and noticed that I didn't even have my phone. She looked at me and dropped her head.

"Carter, I think Mea left her phone in the car or something, it's a lot going on right now," I heard her say. "We should be leaving here in a minute. I will have her call you back."

I watched her wait for a response and hang up. I was just ready to go. I didn't want to have to deal with Carter right now. I had enough going on. I looked at the doorway to the bathroom, and the tears started flowing again. I really couldn't be here any longer, I didn't want to throw up no more and now all I could smell is death.

"Is that all the questions because I really think I need my friend needs to lay down." Jakirra turned to the detective.

"We do need an official statement if y'all can come down to the station," he said as he searched for something in his pockets.

"But I'm sure you can come down tomorrow and do that."
Jakirra nodded and he handed her two business cards.

"If you can think of anything or hear anything please don't hesitate to give me a call. Day or night, I have my cell on the card also."

We collected our things and headed for the door; I knew this situation was far from over. The elevator ride down was silent, when we walked outside the news crew was setting up for a story. They must have been tipped off of some foul play found at the scene because I was sure I heard one of the reporters say something about young girl found strangled in the tub in a nice suburban neighborhood. At that moment, I wondered if we should've made her vanish like Ant. No body no case, she would have become another missing person to add to the wall.

Carter

I somehow convinced Cartier and Ced to go back to the city and handle the business. That allowed me to meet with Mario and take care of business with him. I took the nigga Ant's car to get rid of it and I had arranged for Monea to pick me up at a supermarket ten minutes from where I was meeting the connect. I hadn't really thought about what to do about Monea and her bullshit she attempted to participate in with that fuck nigga Ant. To be honest, I had a feeling I was going to have to fuck him up, so it was a good thing he was dead. I merged right onto the 90 west exit ramp. I looked at the time, Mario should have either beat me here or was pulling up at the same time. Mario asked me to meet him at this warehouse, he claimed that's where the money was at. Whether he was on some bullshit or not I had my steel with me just in case.

This nigga Mario was late, Monea had called twenty times in the last thirty minutes. She was bugging and trying to rush me. I didn't have time for her nagging shit, I was trying to get this money. People failed to realize how much I hated extra shit.

"Aye," Mario said, tapping my window.

I didn't even notice he had pulled up. I knew he wasn't rushing me either knowing his ass was the one late.

"Took yo ass long enough. You're looking a little empty handed too," I said, hopping out the car. "This is the reason we set times so the other person ain't just out here waiting, looking hot as fuck."

Mario smirked and still didn't say a word. I continued to follow him to a storage bin, where I watched him put in a code

28-09.

"Where are your brothers? I never knew one come without the others," he finally said, placing a bag on the cart.

"They had other business to handle. You're looking kinda short ain't you?" I looked over at the single bag. "That's not what we talked about yesterday."

"See I went back to tell them the offer and my people said they were unable to successfully do business that way. I got the drugs we first agreed on," he said, sitting in the only chair in the storage area. "That's why I was counting on all of you being here today."

"Man, Mario you on some fuck shit, that's not what we talked about yesterday. Why waste a trip if you planned on playing games." I was furious.

"It's all business. This game isn't for everybody and maybe it's time for you and your brothers to hang up the towel. Allow me to come in and take over."

"Are you smoking the shit your selling us too?" I chuckled. "The game ain't for you, brah. Fuck niggas like you don't even deserve to be in the game. You definitely don't know shit about it."

"You know what I do know?"

"What's that, big homie?"

"Your brothers is gon' miss dey brother." Mario pulled out 380 handguns.

I already had a feeling this was how the shit was about to play out. I knew when I pulled up, and he wasn't here that I was going to have to kill this nigga. I knew when I hopped out the car and he looked empty handed I was going to have to murder this nigga. Before he could get out his word, I reached under my shirt and pulled out my steel and started bussing. The shots rang out like loud fireworks.

Pop Pop Pop Pop Pop

It was either me or him, and I'm always about my business. I walked up to him and shot him in dead in the face. I tore that storage up; this nigga had the money and shit here.

I couldn't stick around too long, I found five-hundred thousand in the trunk and I found a couple bricks stashed behind some fake ass boxes. I knew nothing good was going to come from this. But this would hold us over until we could find another connect. My only issue was explaining all this bullshit to my brothers. I knew Cartier wouldn't say too much shit. Ced on the other hand he was definitely going to have some bullshit to say about unnecessary heat. I couldn't worry about none of that shit. I just needed to make it to this hoe Monea and get out of sight.

***

I never thought I was would be so happy to see Monea's face. Even though, I knew she tried to play me, I still needed this hoe. It was like a sigh of relief once I was on my way back to the spot.

"What took you so long? I got worried," she finally said as she turned down the music.

I smirked. I just bet her ass was worried. I wanted to ask her about the Ant shit, but it was a time and place for everything and right now wasn't it. I looked at her again, which I knew she was waiting on an answer, I shook my head.

"Shit just was taking longer den I expected, that's all."

I kept it short and sweet. She didn't need to know no extra shit.

"So, you couldn't call. You couldn't send me a text or nothing. I'm sittin' in the middle of no man's land, looking about weird as fuck sittin' in the car!" she said sarcastically.

"Nope, I told you shit took longer den I expected. You were fine," I said, giving her the side eye.

She poked her lip out and turned the music back up, this was an argument she wasn't winning today. I didn't have time for her shit. I still had to figure out how the fuck I was going to explain to my brothers that I robbed and killed our only connect. Those couple of bricks that I found wasn't going to last us long at all, our clientele had doubled times ten since last year. The ride home was a silent one. I definitely needed it. I didn't feel like doing nothing other than enjoy my ride.

I really didn't have time to chill with Monea, once we got back to the city, I had her drop me to the hood. I needed to figure out where I was going to stash these bricks. We never kept a full inventory of the products we had where we trapped at. So just in case, it was never nothing over a misdemeanor. We didn't need any extra heat. Something about today felt good. Ced and Cartier was already down at the spot.

"The man of the hour," Cartier said, dapping me up as I walked in. "Where you been at?"

"I had to put this play down. I need to holla at ya'll about a few things too," I sat the bag in front of the both of them. "We gotta get another connect."

They both looked at each other and then at the bag. I knew they were confused.

"What happened to the other connect, brah?" Ced asked, shaking his head.

I knew he already knew why we needed a new connect. He just wanted to hear how reckless the situation was. I really didn't have time for his shit either. I made a call and I did what needed to be done. Shit, them niggas was trying to play us like we were some average corner boys. They definitely had us confused with some other niggas.

"That fuck nigga was trying to play us out. Shit got ugly and shit ya'll ain't no dummy, I did what I had to do. Now what's in the bag," I shifted their attention back on the black bag.

"This is what we really need to talk about and the money. That's what's important right now."

"It's really too much killing going on in one fucking week for me," Cartier laughed sarcastically. "Ced, at least we benefit from this killing. What do we have in this bag of goodies?"

That's why I fucked with Cartier. Don't get me wrong, I loved all my brothers the same but my baby brother, Cartier, he was a lot like me. We both always looked at the bigger picture. We focused on what it was instead of what it wasn't. Ced on the other hand always wanted to be like the father figure, the I told you so type of shit. I didn't have time for the fatherly lectures today. I still had to go home and give my own lecture to my dingy ass girl who allowed unnecessary fuck shit to happen. I opened the bag to expose to bricks and the money.

"Damn, brah. How much is that?" Cartier asked, moving the bricks to the side and focusing on the money.

"Maybe a little over 500k. The bricks we can divide between the guys and they can get it out, it's the same pack from before so I know it's some good." I smirked. "Only issue I see, figuring out who we gon' fuck with."

"Brah, them bricks ain't gon last us long. Yeah I see you got the money, but the money never been an issue. You can't be just fucking shit up and expect me to make miracles happen. Now I gotta call these muthafuckas and make nice because right now we need them," Ced bitched.

"Ain't no making nice, that nigga Mario was gon' kill me. They planned to take us out the game. He said it out his own mouth. He was tryin' to short us and I wasn't having it. I made a call, and you should respect it," I shot back. "Everything doesn't have to go through you. I know you would love for us to do so, but sometimes we have to make our own calls. You can't expect us to do that with every business situation."

"I'm not saying consult me with your every move, but a decision to completely kill our plug, was a bad call," he continued to argue.

"And the moment I picked up my phone or did anything other than what the fuck I did, I wouldn't be standing right here in front of ya'll now. I did what I knew was best at the time."

"Only problem I have with the situation is where are we gonna find another plug at, on top of that, on such a short notice?" Cartier finally stepped in. "We all know these few bricks won't last us that long. Maybe a week tops.

"Shit you're right, but in the meantime, we can also put into motion these other projects, we could be looking into opening our own shit up, we've been talking about going legit with some shit. Why not start now." I just threw out some ideas.

"Ain't shit wrong with that, we can start doing all that, but we still need a plug, we still gotta produce the product to the streets. It's still left on me." Ced continued with his fatherly rant. "Ya'll don't get it, when ya'll do crazy shit like this, I nine times outta ten have to clean up the mess. This wouldn't be an issue if you didn't lose your head, and went alone."

I waved him off. I didn't even ask him to look for the connect though. I sat in the corner and looked at my phone. I had completely tuned him out now.

I hadn't talked to La'Mea since we left the house, and she didn't call either. She knew that I was still pissed at her. The shit she pulled with Ant; I wasn't fucking feeling at all. It light weight made me want to stop fucking with her, but I really loved her ass. I went to our text messages, the silence between us wasn't normal, we still had to discuss my baby growing inside her.

Man, where you at?

I hit send and looked up at Ced who was still trying to lecture Cartier. I honestly think he just liked to hear himself talk. I laughed to myself. The vibration of my phone made me jump a little.

Bae: I thought you needed some space. I don't wanna fight with you. I really do need to talk to you.

I felt like I read the text fifty times. La'Mea had her way of acting like she knew me. She knew though it was a chance if she texted or called me before I was ready to talk to her, it wasn't going to happen.

You didn't answer my question?

It was really only two places she could been, but after the sneaky shit, she needed to build her trust back up with me.

Bae: At the house. I didn't go to work today. I wasn't feeling good. Are you coming home?

I quickly replied.

Idk yet. I'ma call you in a minute.

I looked up again at my brothers. I stood up and headed to the bathroom. I didn't wanna get sucked into Ced's lecture. I was ready to go.

"Well I haven't been home. I guess it's time for me to tend to my problems there," I said, walking from the bathroom.

“You ain’t talked to La’Mea since that day?” Cartier asked confused.

“On some real shit, brah, I couldn’t even look at that girl. I know she wasn’t lying about being pregnant by me. I’m just ain’t feeling the fact that she was meeting with this nigga behind my back.” I shook my head. “That shit just ain’t sittin’ right with me. I mean you can’t tell me that she is that damn gullible.”

“I mean I’m not gonna lie, Jakirra said that the nigga Ant kept making it seem like they couldn’t speak over the phone, that’s why she took them with her,” Ced explained.

“Her ass should have still called me. She knew better than dat shit. Then she was acting like she couldn’t talk and shit at the house. I felt like she was trying to play me like a fuck nigga and I just wasn’t feeling that shit at all.”

They all knew me, and she knew for a fact that when I found out, I wasn’t going to have an understanding no matter who said what. She didn’t come to me first and she knows don’t shit move unless I gave the okay. If anybody knew me, she did.

“I mean shit for real brah, she did us a favor. The nigga Ant was definitely gonna be a problem. That nigga was going to end up dead anyway. And shit he was tryin’ to get on with us, this could work. We could double back like wit was gon’ fuck with dude and now he’s nowhere to be found. Tell the streets like we only wanna work with him, so now nobody else from their crew can try to step in for him. Shit that’s one less weird ass nigga we gotta worry about,” Cartier continued. “This wasn’t really a bad thing. The only thing is they can’t slip up and tell nobody.”

Cartier wasn’t wrong. I was kind of plotting putting the bullet in the nigga’s head after he tried to be funny by basically saying he fucked my bitch. I was never gon’ put that weird ass nigga on my payroll, let alone front him some shit. My phone vibrated again; it was La’Mea again.

Bae: De’Asia is dead bae. I really need to talk to you. I’m freaking out. I really need you, she’s really dead. I read the text message at least four times. What the fuck happened that fast? Did she lose it and kill her own best friend? I looked up my brothers, who were not looking at me. I knew they caught my reaction and were waiting to find out what the fuck had me so stunned.

"What's up, brah?" Ced finally broke the awkward silence.

"Shit, I'ma call ya'll in a minute." I was headed out the door.

I didn't even text La'Mea back. I had so many questions.

It felt like it took me forever to get to the house, I took all the side streets, and I still felt like it took me forever just to get to the house. I swear I sat outside for an extra ten minutes just really trying to collect all the patience that required me to deal with this bullshit. I just could never really prepare myself for anything that comes with my love.

***

"La'Mea," I called out coming through the back door. "Bae."

"Yeah," she walked in the kitchen holding the paper.

"What's up with you? What do you mean De'Asia is dead?"

I didn't waste time on shit. She had a lot of explaining to do, and I wasn't trying to hear shit but the truth at this point.

"You haven't talked to your brother?" she said, placing the newspaper down so I could see the article on De'Asia.

Young female found dead in her bathroom.

The shit made the front page. La'Mea and Jakirra were mentioned as her friends that found her. The police had no suspects and was reaching out to the public for leads. I shook my head and looked back at La'Mea.

"What you mean did I talk to my brother?"

"He was there. He killed my best friend," La'Mea cried out. "It's all my fault. Cartier overheard Jakirra and I talking the other day. Jakirra was telling me that De'Asia was complaining about not being able to sleep and talking about telling on us. We planned to go over there and talk to her, but when we got there, Cartier was there and De'Asia was dead. He made us stick to the story that we found her. I didn't know what to do. I felt like I had no choice. I killed Ant and that's the reason why De'Asia is dead."

I watched her cry. I wanted to comfort her, but I didn't

budge. I was now confused; I had just seen Cartier and he said nothing. I was now wondering if Ced knew about this too. It was too many secrets and bullshit going on around me and it was like I was oblivious to it all.

"So, let me get this straight, you're telling me that Cartier killed De'Asia?" I had to sit down all this was too much.

"Yes bae, he drowned her. We walked in right after he did it. I felt like I didn't have no other choice. Like he killed her because she kept talking about telling," she added.

"Man, it's too many fucking secrets that's the first problem, and when I called why didn't ya'll tell me that? Why didn't you call me when you got there and see what the fuck happened? This shit is really starting to make me feel a certain kinda way." I was pissed. "You're my bitch, you don't make no decisions or calls without checking with me first. Do you understand?"

She nodded.

"All I want you to do is go to work, take care of home, and get ready for this baby. Don't do shit else, La'Mea. Now what did Cartier say to you when ya'll found him in De'Asia's house?"

"He basically said he did it because she told him she was going to go to the police, and he wasn't going to jail for that bitch." She tried to control her tears.

I dropped my head in my hands. These muthafuckas was just killing shit, I mean I understood each situation, and yes shit has to be handled, but damn not like this.

"La'Mea, you shoulda came to me when that nigga Ant called you, it's no excuse why you didn't. This one wrong decision caused De'Asia to be dead. If you woulda told me what you were up to instead of lying like you did, this coulda went so differently." I shook my head again. I was irritated. "I'm about to go out to Wendy's and I will be back. Lay down or something, don't do shit."

She didn't say a word, she turned and walked away. I was eventually going to make it to Wendy's, but first I needed to go back down to the hood and talk to my brothers. I grabbed the front page of the newspaper and shoved it in my pocket.

***

It was like my brothers were waiting on me to return. I knew they were waiting on me to tell them what was going on.

"Cartier, is it something that we need to talk about?" I asked as soon as I locked the door behind me.

Cartier didn't say a word, he immediately looked at the floor. Ced looked as confused as I did not too long ago.

"What's going on?" Ced asked, looking at both of us. "What the hell did I miss?"

"Shit that's what I'm tryin' to figure out. Jakirra ain't tell you what happen? It's all over the front page of the fucking newspaper," I said pulling it out my pocket.

They both reached for the paper and Cartier sat down.

"Jakirra ain't tell me shit about this. Who killed her? Jakirra and La'Mea? Cartier?" He started guessing.

"Our little brother!" I spat. "Cartier why the fuck didn't you say nothing? Why didn't you call one of us? You took it upon yourself to kill this damn girl and den you had Jakirra and La'Mea lie to the fucking police? What were you thinking, I mean shit was you thinking?"

"Man, that bitch said she was going to the fucking police. I'm not going to jail for NOBODY!" he yelled. "That bitch was a liability and we can't afford liabilities. I made a call just like you made that call to kill our plug. We both did what we thought was right at the time. Don't come in here tryin' to play daddy because this shit wouldn't have happened it La'Mea pregnant ass didn't kill Ant. We really shoulda killed that hoe when we got rid of Ant, then the bullshit wouldn't have made the first page."

"Cartier, you shouldn't have killed the girl. She wasn't gon' tell." Ced was disgusted. "Ya'll are being reckless, it's just too much fucking killing going on. Now what if the police go after these two dummies. That's another headache I don't want to deal with, brah. I hate that we have to find a new plug. I hate that we have to keep this De'Asia and Ant shit on the hush, hush. This shit is unnecessary."

"Brah, she was gon' fucking tell, she told me, she said some shit about no sleeping and all this other bullshit. I just couldn't take that chance. Even if La'Mea and Jakirra talked to her, she was still gon' tell. The bitch had to go. I don't feel bad, I really don't care. The game just ain't for everybody, some people are going to be killed, robbed, fucked up, and some more shit. And like I said I made a call and that's just that."

I could go back and forth with Cartier all day. He didn't see shit wrong with De'Asia because she threatened his freedom and I understood that. I didn't have a problem with none of that. What I had a problem with is the fact everybody keeping fucking secrets and the police got involved. If we kill some shit, they go missing, not to be found, that's just how we moved. I didn't do that with that weird ass nigga Mario, I wanted them to know it was a drug deal gone bad.

"So La'Mea told you?" Cartier continued.

"Did you think she wasn't?"

"Nah, I knew she was going to most likely tell you," he said. Ced just kept shaking his head. I knew he was ready to give us a whole speech, but I still had to get La'Mea's food. Cartier knew it too, on my way out the door, he followed.

"Brah. my bad on not letting you know about the De'Asia shit, I did what I thought was the right thing. Dead people can't tell shit, and I know her weak ass was definitely going to the police," Cartier said still walking behind me.

"Look brah, I'm not knocking you for making a call, I understand that. I believe that hoe was going to go to the police too, it was just a matter of time. I just wanted to hear it from you and not my bitch and definitely not from the newspaper. That's all I'm saying." I slowed up so we could be side by side. "Brah, just next time when you make a move, just make sure you let me know."

We dapped up and went our separate ways. I couldn't be mad at him though. Shit, we all was making moves for the good I guess.

La'Mea

I didn't even want to argue with Carter. This baby was kicking my ass and I had to mentally prepare myself for De'Asia's funeral. I wasn't ready. Tears rolled down my face. I placed the picture of me, De'Asia, and Jakirra facedown. My best friend was really gone, and I only could blame myself. Yes, Cartier killed De'Asia, but he wouldn't have had to if I didn't kill Ant. My momma always told me with every action, it's a reaction. My phone started vibrating breaking my train of thought. Unknown caller. I rolled my eyes, I didn't have time, all before I even knew who it really was.

"Hello."

"Hello, you have a prepaid call from Jeez, an inmate at Cuyahoga County Jail, this call is subject for recording and monitoring. If you wish to accept this call press 5, if you wish to block this call and all future calls from this inmate and facility press 0." The recording played out.

I wanted to press 0 so bad. I didn't have time for his shit today. I knew he saw the newspaper and was probably calling to check on me. I pressed 5.

"Thank you for using County Calls, you may begin your conversation," the recording message replied.

"Yes, Jeez," I said dryly.

"Damn, I miss you too. How are you? I heard about De'Asia?"

"I'm dealing. What can I do for you?" I said, cutting right to the point. I didn't have time for Carter coming in.

"I know our last conversation didn't go good, La'Mea, I mean but what do you expect. My niggas telling me that you fucking with the same dude I beat your ass about. So, you mean to tell me that still after it all you kept fucking with this nigga behind my back? How fucked up is that?"

"Look, Jeez, you told me numerous times that I wasn't your bitch, you played on me and when I finally give you a taste of your own medicine you're sick. You had my heart, you took my shit and ripped it up and spit on my shit."

"That don't mean fuck with another nigga, La'Mea. You were supposed to stay solid. You weren't supposed to give my pussy away to another nigga. You fucking knew better. You didn't even have the decency to wait til' a nigga did his time. Like, bitch, I could have never had your whole heart, the fuck you mean?"

"Jeez, we've been through his conversation, I'm not about to keep going through this every time you call me. YOU'RE NEVER GONE CHANGE, AND I'M NEVER GONE BE THAT GIRL FOR YOU. So stop sitting here trying to make it seem like those was your intentions because it wasn't." He had pissed me off as usual trying to act like the fucking victim. "I walked away not because I didn't love you no more, but because I knew you didn't love me the same. You didn't want it as bad as I did."

Jeez was silent for the first time. He knew everything that I was saying was the truth. He knew he had my heart, and he knew he was the reason why we didn't work. He wanted his cake and wanted to eat it too, and that shit didn't work anymore. The situation with Carter was so much better, but I never had to question his love and respect for me.

"You talking about all this shit, but when you needed me, I was there. When you tried to kill yourself, I was there with you, I didn't leave or run away. I knew you were damaged, and I still fucked wit you. That should tell you something about the love I have for you. Yeah I fucked with other hoes but come on what nigga don't. I'm pretty sure your Mr. Perfect has fucked with some hoes. I know for a fact that he has," he argued.

My stomach was beginning to turn, the things Ant said about Carter meeting a hoe at the hotel brought chills down my spine. The thoughts of all the blood and his body being stuffed into the furnace was too much right now. I felt sick, I dropped the phone and ran to the bathroom. I hated throwing up. I felt like my insides were coming out. When I finally made it to back to the phone, the call had ended. I was praying that he didn't call back; I didn't want to deal with him anymore. I buried my head in my pillows and started to cry. I didn't know what to do at this point, nothing was going right; I had killed someone that I once loved because he planned to kill someone I was in love with. Was I wrong? Was Jeez right, did he really have my heart? Why was it so easy to walk away from him? Did I fall out of love with him before I started dealing with Carter? It was so many unanswered questions that I had. I hadn't talked to Jakirra since De'Asia's death, and I knew I would eventually have to deal with her sooner than later. I knew she blamed me too; she just loved me enough not to say anything.

***

Waking up to Carter sitting at the edge of the bed, rubbing my stomach, was comforting. I knew he was pissed at me about the Ant and De'Asia shit. I just needed him to understand that Ant was an accident. He charged at me, all I wanted to do was call Carter and warn him. What was I supposed to do. I was afraid he was going to hurt me or my unborn child. He already expressed how he was about to have the person I loved killed.

"Bae, have you talked to De'Asia's family. I mean how are ya'll planning to stand in these peoples faces knowing what really happened to their daughter," Carter asked, handing me my food.

"Yeah I've spoken to them a little. I really can't stand in front of anyone right now knowing everything started from some shit that was self-defense. She got mixed up in a bad situation. She was never supposed to get hurt. This shit is my fault. I shoulda never went to meet Ant, I'm sorry."

"First, I want you to understand, niggas know not to play with me, that weird ass nigga was gon' get his regardless, no matter who did it. Bitch was going to catch one. I just wish you would have told me. That sneaky shit almost made me stop fucking with you, with you having the baby and all. I don't like that sneaky shit

Mea and you know that." He just shook his head.

"Bae, I swear I was about to call you though, he grabbed me and charged at me. It was just a natural reaction because I was scared. I was in there alone."

"And again, why didn't you make De'Asia and Jakirra come in? You chose to be in there with that nigga by yourself." He completely cut me off. "I don't think he woulda tried that shit if you had them in the house with you."

"I wasn't even planning on being in there long though," I protested. "Like everything spiraled out of control so quickly. I was so scared. I didn't even know if he was really dead. I never touched him after he fell to the ground. It's like everything after that felt like an out of body experience."

Just the thought of me killing Ant sent me running back to the bathroom again; I couldn't get the images out my head. Carter walked to the doorway of our bathroom.

"Are you cool?" he tossed me a face cloth. "You definitely need to eat something, throwing up like that."

I didn't even want to see food, but I knew if I declined the food it would be a whole thing about staying healthy. I picked myself up off the toilet bowl and laid across the bed. Carter placed the food in my face. I knew I was going to throw up again.

"So, when is the funeral and when is your next doctor's appointment?"

"I don't know. I'm supposed to go over De'Asia's mom house in a few, I just don't feel up to it. And I have to call, it was so crowded at my last appointment I just left," I replied, picking over the food.

"I will take you to her mom's house when you're ready. Call and make your appointment, and stop picking over the food, La'Mea. Eat the food now," he said before disappearing downstairs.

I did what I was told, well most of what I was told. I shoved the food into the bathroom garbage and laid back down. I had time for a nap, that's the only thing that put my mind and body at ease.

***

It was awkward being in De'Asia mom's house. Carter held my hand as we walked through the living and dining room. It was like she added tons of De'Asia's pictures to her house since she was killed. Jakirra was sitting at the table already, I knew she was broken. She looked better than I did; she had a fresh sew-in, mani and pedi set, and her face was beat to a T. I was walking in with my tired ass sew-in, brushed into a ponytail. I needed a fill so bad, and we ain't even going to speak on how my toes were looking. I didn't put on no lip gloss and I didn't have my lashes, and may I say I never go anywhere without my lashes on fleek.

"La'Mea, can I get you something to eat or drink, baby?" De'Keisha asked, pulling out some extra chairs. "De'Asia had told us you were pregnant. I think that's the last conversation I had with my baby sister."

De'Keisha was De'Asia's older sister. They were one year apart and very close since De'Keisha had found out she was pregnant five months ago. De'Asia was excited to become an auntie. De'Keisha held her stomach and cried. Jakirra looked at the floor and I looked over at Carter. This was weird, didn't know if it was right to comfort her. She just kept asking why someone would kill her sister. I wanted to speak up and give them closure, but I knew that wasn't even an option. She would be just another case gone cold.

"I just hope my baby didn't suffer; I just pray she went quick." Her mother cleared her throat. "She was supposed to come, she told me she needed to talk to me about something important, but she never said what it was."

"It was probably the reason why she had been so distant lately. Not returning calls. The one day I did talk to her, she said she hadn't been sleeping. My sister was going through something," De'Keisha added. "The police said ya'll talked to her and ya'll was the ones that found her?"

She was fishing, and it was okay because they were trying to figure out what happened to the person they loved. Jakirra placed her hands over her eyes, like she could picture the day all over again, but she still said nothing. Carter nudged me to speak up. I just glared at him.

"Yes, she had told us she wasn't sleeping, we were supposed to get together that day to talk about it, trying to just give her a chance to vent and when we got there she wasn't answering." I tried to leave out anything about the killing of Ant. "We had to use the spare to come in."

"So ya'll did talk to her? Both of you?" De'Keisha asked for clarification.

"Yes, we were on three way. You know that's how we always talk."

"Yes, you girls stayed with my lines tied up. I remember yelling at ya'll everyday about that all the time," her mother said, picking up a picture of the three of us when we were kids. "I just wanna know why they took my baby. We can't afford to bury my baby. I don't want to."

De'Keisha walked over to her mom and hugged her and cried. Tears continued to fall down my face as well. I looked over towards Jakirra who still her eyes had covered. This was so fucked up. What mother wants to bury their baby?

"Whatever ya'll need, I got it. De'Asia was family. She is family. Just let La'Mea know the cost and I will send the money. Don't worry about nothing," Carter assured them.

De'Asia's mom graciously thanked Carter for offering to pay for the funeral. I thought she was going to decline. I knew for a fact just because my nigga said he was paying for it; she was going to make sure she got the most expensive shit.

"Well, I have to go, I will call the church and make the arrangements," Jakirra finally spoke up. "Call me if you need me to do anything. I took off for a little while so I will be home. What colors would you like to wear and what day?"

"Let's do De'Asia's favorite color black and purple, and we can have it Friday. I think that gives us enough time to get things ready." De'Asia mom sat at the table and grabbed my hands. "I want you to write something for me, something on the back. You know De'Asia supported your writing since you were kids."

"I'm pretty sure that I can put something together for my best." I smiled.

"Well get at me with the price, I have some business to handle," Carter stood up and gave everybody a hug. "Come on, bae."

I was happy Carter was ready to leave, Friday was around the corner and I still needed to put something together for her obituary. I don't know how I was going to be able to pull that off, but I had no choice.

***

I felt like a zombie walking around the house the days approaching the funeral. I managed to pull myself together to write her a nice poem for the back of the obituary. My stomach grew a tad bit, so Carter and I planned to go to the mall to pick up something for the funeral.

"Bae, it's going to be too hot for us to be in all black," Carter said, getting ready to go. "Why aren't you ready yet?"

"Bae, I'm just not feeling up to it, I don't want to go to the funeral," I complained. "The day is coming fast, and I just don't think I could look at her like that. I don't want to."

"You really don't have a choice at this point bae, now throw this one and let's go. I gotta make a move." He tossed my black pencil skirt, and my white blouse on the bed. "Hurry up too."

I looked at him, he's always talking about I didn't have a choice. I'm pregnant; I really could use this as a perfect excuse not to go. I put my jogging suit on as slow as I could. I didn't want Carter to come back in and I'm wasn't ready either. I dragged my fat ass down the stairs and sat on the couch ready to go.

***

Her funeral was beautiful so many people came out. A lot of people we went to school with came out to say their final goodbyes. It wasn't a dry eye in the building. De'Keisha wanted me and Jakirra to sit in the front row with them. I thought it was okay considering we've been friends forever; we were family in her eyes.

"Have the police contacted you again?" Jakirra whispered.

"No, I haven't checked any of my messages lately though."

"They asked me to come down. They want to go over my statement again, they have a few more questions."

"Just go, stay calm, we didn't do nothing. We really did find her like that. We had nothing to do with it. Calm down," I tried to sound as reassuring as I could. "That's normal. Just talk to them and get it over with because if you don't it will seem like we're hiding something."

Jakirra grabbed my hand and held it tightly. Carter and Ced joined us after a while. I was happy Carter had been supportive of this messed up situation. I knew he still felt a certain kind of way about it all, but he never turned his back on me.

"La'Mea, would you like to say a few things? We can't get up there right now. I can barely think straight," De'Keisha asked, leaning over Carter's lap.

I wanted to tell her no, but considering the circumstances, I stood up and walked to the podium. My heart was so heavy, nobody wanted to hear the lies that was about to come out my mouth. I felt like if I wasn't going to tell them who killed De'Asia, then what was it to say. I closed my eyes and allowed the tears to fall from my face.

"This is so hard for me right now because this wasn't supposed to be the outcome. I'm not supposed to be looking at my best friend in this box. That's exactly what it is. De'Asia, Jakirra, and I are supposed to be getting ready to have baby showers and planning weddings, not sitting in a church with tears in our eyes saying goodbye," the tears were flowing now; it was like the more I wiped my face, the faster the tears rolled down my face. "I can't do this."

It was like no words came out that I understood myself. It was so hot in the church; I could barely hold myself up at the podium. I felt arms wrap around me as I slid to the floor. I couldn't see nor could I move. I reached for my stomach. God what was happening. Was I losing my baby? Was I dying myself? Was this my punishment for getting up there and talking like I had no idea why this happened to my best friend. A part of me was ready to accept whatever was about to come.

***

I had a panic attack. When I woke up, I was in Metro Hospital with a thousand IV's, and a baby monitor. I just knew I died in that church. I didn't want to be here. I wanted to go home; I mean I really wanted everything that had went on in the last past two weeks to be just a memory. I pulled on the IV, causing one of many alarms to go off. Nursing ran in before I could completely sit up.

"La'Mea, please don't pull at those!" Jakirra yelled, coming in behind them.

Carter followed and so did De'Keisha. I was so happy to see them, at the same time I just wanted to get out of there.

"Bae, just calm down; I know you don't wanna be here, but we have to make sure everything is okay with the baby first." Carter was now standing at the end of the bed looking over me.

"I just wanna go home, please bae, just take me home," I cried out.

"Soon as the doctor gives the okay, I promise I will take you home," he assured me.

I heard my phone ring in the distance. Carter walked over and I knew he was debating if he wanted to answer. He picked it up and said hello. From the pause I knew it who it was, Jeez. I didn't utter another world.

Carter

I watched La'Mea breakdown, I've never seen her like this. This situation would have played out a lot differently if everybody wasn't doing their own thing, and making decisions that they felt was right at that moment. I felt like I couldn't get to her fast enough when she started to breakdown. We rushed her straight to the hospital. I knew that was the last place she wanted to be, but at that point she had no other choice. Since she arrived, her phone hadn't stopped ringing. We normally respected each other's privacy, but because she was earning my trust back, wasn't shit private right now. I debated answering her phone, I knew from the caller id it was a jail call.

"Brah, this shit gotta stop. You calling all fuckin' day and shit. What the fuck do you want?" I asked as soon as I accepted the call.

"Oh, this must be bae himself?" Jeez chuckled. "Damn you putting yo foot down finally. Too bad it's too late."

"Look, I don't know what type of weird shit you're into, but I'm not into that. Just stop calling my girl, it's really simple. Ya'll don't have shit to talk about." I wasn't about to keep playing with this nigga.

"Man, she's your bitch by default. I didn't really want her no more. I had no need for her. But honestly I was calling to give her the good news, but shit it can be relayed. The evidence in my case was tampered with, so you know what that means homie," he laughed.

"I don't give a fuck about the shit you're talking about, brah. Just make this your last phone call," I said.

"I don't wanna beef, brah. I was just calling to check on

baby girl with burying her best friend. I guess I will catch her in traffic," Jeez smirked.

"Yep, you do that," I said before handing up.

I knew exactly what Jeez was getting at. I knew when he said they tampered with the evidence that meant it was only a matter of time before he be back out in these streets. He would be just another problem to deal with. I looked over to La'Mea's, she had her hands wrapped around her small belly. I didn't know what was wrong but, I didn't have to say a word about Jeez, La'Mea knew from the look in my eyes that I meant what I said about that being his last call.

"I will pick you up when you are discharged, that's if and when you are discharged. If you need to call me, call from that phone," I pointed at the hospital phone beside her bed. "La'Mea just do as I'm saying, and we won't have any issues."

I didn't give her a chance to say shit. I placed her phone in my back pocket and walked out. I didn't have time for shit right now. My first priority right now was making sure we had a new plug. It was time for me to clean up the mess we all somehow created.

***

"Can I have my phone back now?" Le'Mea asked standing in front of the bed with her arms resting on her now rounded belly.

"Hey beautiful," I ignored her.

"Bae, I need to check my phone, I haven't been at work, I need to make some phone calls, everything. Please give me back my phone, bae."

It was kind of cute watching her pregnant face beg. I handed her my phone, and smiled.

"Call and check your messages, you don't have anything else going on."

"Why can't I have my phone back?" she shouted.

"Do you wanna check your shit or not," I cut her off. "I mean if not give me back my phone and stop yelling, no stress remember."

"You're trying to be funny," she rolled her eyes checked her messages.

I knew she would see things my way. I watched her pace the floor, I tried to listen just in case Jeez didn't take my warning serious, but I couldn't catch the different voices. La'Mea froze and immediately looked over at me. I leaned up and gave her all my attention. She pressed a button and put the phone on speaker.

"Hi La'Mea, this is Detective Jones, I've been reassigned to your friends De'Asia's case, I've been trying to get in touch with you. I really need you to come down to the station for a follow on up on your statement that you and Ms. Jakirra gave at the crime scene. I know that this is a hard time for you, but I really need you to be available as soon as possible. Give me a call at 216-662-3060. Talk to you soon."

The voicemail ended. I could see the fear in La'Mea's eyes. This wasn't what she expected. I knew she was about to panic. I took a deep sigh and snatched my phone. This was the shit I was afraid of. La'Mea sat at the edge of the bed, I knew it was more to this shit. I was just afraid to ask.

"What?" I finally broke the silence.

"They called Jakirra too. She told me at the funeral." She dropped her head. "Do you think they know? Do you think they know what we know?"

"Don't be fucking stupid La'Mea, as long as nobody said shit, the shit happened just like ya'll said it did. This is why ya'll shoulda fucking called me. Call Jakirra ass over her now, I will call my brothers. We gotta make sure this shit doesn't go left."

I was so fucking pissed off. We didn't have time for the police to really be involved. We both headed in different directions. I just knew shit wasn't nothing nice that we're up against. It was one thing with Mario's people, we knew them and what to expect. The police on the other hand, we couldn't be sloppy, everybody needed to be on the same page. We had no room for fuck ups.

***

Everybody got to the house in great timing. I didn't have time for excuses or extra shit.

"So, what the police wanna talk to them, all they gotta do is stick to the same story. What's so fucking hard about that," Cartier argued.

"See that's what you're misunderstanding. The case was getting cold, they brought in fresh eyes to catch what they think the other detective missed. Pay attention, this shit can disappear or leave us in some shit we can't get out of!" Ced explained. "Now do you see the reason why I said what I said the other day."

"I swear I think ya'll are making this more than what it has to be. They just wanna see if they girls' stories will change," Cartier repeated. "Nobody seen me when I went in, it's no cameras. Come on ya'll know these muthafuckas are fishing. We all know what's going on."

"Cartier just shut up and fucking listen man." I finally got fed up. "Even if they are fishing you need everything to go smoothly. We don't have no time for anyone to poke holes in anything."

"I think they've been watching me too," Jakirra chimed in.

"What? Baby, why didn't you tell me?" Ced hated being the last to know shit.

"I really don't know for sure, but I've caught myself feeling as if someone was following me. I know a lot of times when I feel something I'm not wrong but what if they have been watching us?" she continued.

"Well technically we really didn't do nothing, it's exactly like we said, we found her," Le'Mea cried out. "We didn't kill our best friend, that's all we have to say."

"That's not the problem, what ya'll are saying isn't the problem, realize it's a whole different ball game once your down in that hell hole. It isn't about the statement y'all gave, it's the fact that they feel like y'all know more than what y'all are telling them. Understand this ain't no shit ya'll see in movies, this shit gets serious." I tried to explain. "So, no it's not about that being your best friend, no it's not about ya'll really not doing nothing. It's about them, they want to one of ya'll to crack, the police ain't trying to help remember that."

"He's not lying, this is what they do. And it's not going to be like it was at De'Asia's apartment. They will put ya'll in two different rooms. They are gonna start asking questions, some questions ya'll going to think, like what does this have to do with this situation? Then they will ask you the same questions in several different ways. Your head will hurt, and you will get tired and that's what they plan to do. This is how they get you. And because ya'll are bitches," Ced paused. La'Mea and Jakirra glared at him for using the word bitches. I knew they were ready to kill him. He didn't leave room for them to jump in.

"Because ya'll are bitches, they gon' use that shit to their advantage. They gon' tell La'Mea if she's lying, she's gonna have her baby in jail. Shit they may tell Jakirra that La'Mea already told them that you both knew exactly who killed De'Asia but she fears the life of her child. They are gonna tell you that they will place ya'll in witness protection and all ya'll have to do is tell the truth." Ced shook his head.

"I would never tell on Cartier doe." La'Mea rolled her eyes. "We are family, the very blood that's running through your blood is running through my child's blood too. What type of disloyal shit would that be?"

"I mean shit you say that now, Jakirra can scream the same shit, but trust it's a whole different play once they have your downtown," Ced replied.

"So, what? Do we not go down there and talk to them? I mean let me know exactly what you're saying Ced?" Jakirra jumped up.

"What I'm saying when ya'll go down there, it won't be alone."

"Are you going too?" she asked.

"No boo, ya'll will take ya'll lawyers with you. Where do you think I was getting at?" he shot back.

"Wait," La'Mea said confused. "Getting a lawyer on what grounds? I mean why, especially when we are supposed to be showing that we are innocent."

"What's the point? You're not innocent bae, I mean shit

you're the last person that should be screaming innocence right now," I chuckled. "From now on everybody will conduct clean business ethics. Nothing is to be moved, pushed, or pulled without a group discussion. Are we all clear?"

They all agreed. I knew Ced and I wasn't finished, I knew he was ready to spazz out about all this shit, but right now it wasn't the time. We needed to get the girls the best lawyers in the city and make sure they were locked down tight when they went to see Detective Jones.

***

La'Mea

Carter had gotten us the best lawyer's in the city. Craig Worthery and company were the best in the city. I even google them, five stars across the board. Every case they've come into contact with had been a success. I knew right then that this situation was serious. I had called Detective Jones first thing Monday morning to set up something. I didn't want to drag it out any longer than it needed to. Our lawyer's told us that they would meet us down at the justice center Tuesday around noon, and let us know it was okay to ride together. Jakirra volunteered to drive, I didn't feel up to driving anyway, this pregnancy was kicking my ass literally.

***

"La'Mea come on we're gonna be late!" Jakirra yelled outside in between the blowing of her horn.

She knew that was one of my biggest pet peeves. Don't blow outside for me, either call or simply get out and knock. That's how niggas picked up hoes they didn't care nothing about. She wasn't my nigga and I wasn't a hoe but shit I still didn't like it.

"Stop that shit, I'm coming," I yelled as I locked the front door. "I hate that shit!"

Jakirra said nothing, she waited till I was good, and she pulled off. The ride downtown seemed so long. The closer we got to the station, the more jittery I got.

"Are you ready for this?" Jakirra asked completely turning off the music.

"I mean do I really have a choice to be ready or not?" I shook my head. "I know this is all my fault and if you blame me, I understand."

"I can't blame nobody; I just want this to be over. We have already lost a good friend; we don't need to lose our freedom. We got this La'Mea."

She was right, it was no time to dwell on the past, we needed to make this right in order to move on. I knew from the time we walked into the justice center that all the prepping that we did was nothing compared to what was exactly about to happen. Our lawyers met us at the check in point. As we walked into the double doors that read, "Cleveland's Detective's Unit."

"Good afternoon how may we help you," the receptionist asked upon our entrance.

"Yes, our clients have a meeting this afternoon with Detective Jones," Mr. Daniels said.

"Oh, right this way.." she uttered as she walked us down a narrow hallway. "Mr. Daniels you and your client will wait in this room, and Mr. Smith you and your client will wait right across the hall.

She smiled and closed the door behind each of us. I felt like I was being locked in a small box and they planned to throw away the key. I needed Carter here with me. I was starting to get the feeling I had at the church.

"Is everything okay?" Mr. Daniels asked, placing his hands

on my shoulder..

"I just need to make a phone call that's all, is that okay?" I pulled out my phone.

"Make it quick, and don't say much you never know who's listening." He instructed me.

I nodded, and walked over to the corner and dialed Carter.

"Damn bae ya'll done der already?" he asked on the first ring.

"Bae I feel sick like I did at the church. I'm shaking, I can't do this. I don't wanna relive that day again," I cried.

"La'Mea, listen to me, this has to happen, you will be fine, take a deep breath, and just relax. It'll all be over, we prayed about this. Now focus." He instructed me. "I will see you when you get home. I love you, La'Mea."

"I love you too."

We said our goodbyes and I sat back down beside Mr. Daniels. It had seemed like they were there forever. Detective Jones, walked in the room beet red, I knew this wasn't gonna be a piece of cake.

"I'm so glad you could find time to come down. I don't know what you needed a lawyer for though," he said, looking at Mr. Daniels company card. "A criminal lawyer at that, I'm confused. Did you do something wrong?"

"My client doesn't talk to anyone without me, no matter what it's for," Mr. Daniels' chimed in.

"So, tell me how long were you and De'Asia best friends? Did you meet her after meeting Jakirra or before?" he continued.

"I met her after I met Jakirra, we have been friends since grade school, we were like family."

"So, you can say you've been involved in De'Asia's personal life, am I right?"

"Yes, you can say that."

"And on you initial statement you said you didn't know anyone that would want to hurt De'Asia am I correct?"

"Yes, that what I said."

I was beginning to sweat. I could feel it, I was afraid that the detective could see it. He rumbled through a few pages, and pulled up something and placed it in front of me. I had a chill that ran down my spine. My baby had started doing carts wheels.

"We recovered some messages from your best friend's cell phone and maybe you can help us understand what exactly it means. Jakirra somehow has no idea, and she's probably lying, but because you were mentioned by name, I'm sure you do." He handed another copy to Mr. Daniels. "See, De'Asia texted someone and told them you did something terrible and she would have to live with the secret for the rest of her life. She also went on to say she was thinking about going to the police. Now that right there is just enough."

"I didn't do anything to my best friend. I swear," I cried out. I couldn't believe this; it was exactly how they said it would be. Mr. Daniels' tried to calm me down, but it was no use.

"I know what you're saying that you didn't do, but from my point a view, it looks like you killed your best friend because she refused to hold this secret that was burdening her. She told you that she was going to tell, so you went to the house and you killed her. Then you called Jakirra to help you clean up the mess, but it was too late. Jakirra had called the police first."

"No, I called the police. That was me, not Jakirra!" I shouted. "You're twisting things, I would never hurt my best friend. I loved her like a sister. Ask Jakirra she will tell you."

"Oh, I plan to, you just sit tight, I will give you a minute with your lawyer," Detective Jones exited the room.

I completely broke down. I knew he was trying to scare me. I didn't do this; I would never hurt or harm De'Asia. She was my best friend, this man had it all wrong.

"La'Mea, I think you should at least hear him out, tell him what secret she was holding on to that had her thinking about going to the police, that's the only way it may clear you. Now they are looking at you as a suspect." Mr. Daniels tried to comfort me.

"No, I didn't do this. She was dead before I got there, I rode with Jakirra. She gotta tell them that. I didn't do this."

I placed my head on the cold table and cried. Everything Ced said would happen was happening. I couldn't believe how they tried to twist the story around. I could only imagine what Jakirra was going through across the hall.

***

My head was hurting. I was hungry and aggravated. Detective Jones had been gone for an hour, I had no service and neither did Mr. Daniels, and I needed to pee on top of it all. He finally came through the door with a sinister smile on his face.

"So, tell me again, what was this secret that De'Asia was holding on tight for you?" he asked again as he sat on the table instead of the chair.

"If your gonna charge my client with De'Asia's murder please do so now. She's pregnant, tired, and hungry. She also needs a restroom. Now you said you wanted to go over her statement, if we're finished then we can leave." Mr. Daniel's motioned me to follow him.

"Oh no La'Mea won't be leaving. La'Mea Black, you're under an arrest for obstruction of justice. You have the right to remain silent. Anything you say can and will be used against you in a court of law. You have the right to an attorney. If you cannot afford an attorney, one will be provided for you. Do you understand these rights I just read to you?" Detective Jones said.

I could barely say yes between my tears. I couldn't believe this shit. Mr. Daniels was saying something, I wasn't worried about him getting me out, I wondered if this was just his way of being a dick with me.

"Once you tell me what I want this will all disappear," he whispered in my ear.

"You're a bastard!" I yelled.

It was no use of all the screaming and yelling. I couldn't help but ask myself, if this was karma. Did I bring this on myself? I couldn't even wipe my own tears.

Once I was booked in, I was finally able to pee and make a phone call. I really didn't like peeing in front of people but shit what choice did I have now. I had to pull myself together before I called Carter. I knew he was already aware of the situation; I was just wondering why they let Jakirra go and not me. All over some text messages, this shit just really didn't seem right. I didn't waste any time, I called Carter first, nobody else mattered. I swear the recording took forever to connect us.

"Bae are you okay?" he asked once he could speak.

"I just wanna go home. I don't wanna be here. Please, bae, come get me," I cried.

"I'm here now, we all are down here waiting to hear something," he replied. "Mr. Daniels called me once you were arrested."

"I don't want him as my lawyer, bae. He let them do this to me," I continued to rant. "He didn't say or do nothing. I had been here all day. How could he not see that they we're going to arrest me? Did they arrest Jakirra?"

"Bae, calm down, they blind sighted ya'll. They got you on some bullshit. They are tryin' to use the text messages De'Asia sent to say that this could have been a motive, but it's not. Jakirra already stated that you both rode together to De'Asia's house and we have an alarm system, it records when alarms are set and unset. You're gonna be fine. Just trust me, I got you."

I tried to believe him; I couldn't help but cry though. I didn't want to be in jail. Who wants to be in jail? My phone call ended, and I was headed back to my cold cell. I was pregnant and in jail, how was I going to explain this to my parents? What did De'Asia's mom think, her best friend was arrested because she could have possible information about her daughter's death and wasn't telling them. I couldn't help to wonder if this would've happened if I was still messing with Jeez? I had so many unanswered questions. I didn't even know where to begin.

Carter

This shit seemed to go from bad to worse. Mr. Daniel's called and informed me that they arrested La'Mea on some bullshit. Something about a text De'Asia sent to someone else, implicating La'Mea did something bad and she was going to go to the police. That shit could've meant anything. She had called once she was booked in and just cried. I was a real hood nigga, but I could even think straight knowing my pregnant girl was locked up over this bullshit. I had been downtown since Mr. Daniels called me, I texted my brothers and told them to get down here, I would need all the support I could get at this point.

"Mr. Daniels did they let her friend go? Jakirra?" I asked, looking around for her.

Just when I mentioned her name, she was being released from the back. She quickly walked over and hugged me tight.

"They're trying to say La'Mea knows something, they asked me about some text messages, and also about how we got to De'Asia'a house. I promise I kept the same story," Jakirra said now shaking. "Where is my best friend, Carter?"

"They arrested her on obstruction of justice. It's some bullshit."

It was a moment of silence. I watched Detective Jones watch us. His white ass knew he had us. Little did he know, we weren't your average street niggas, we were smart, and this shit didn't hold no weight. He was just fucking stalling.

***

It didn't take too long for Cartier and Ced to make it downtown, I knew this was the last place they wanted to be, but at this point we needed to come together and get La'Mea out.

"What are they talking about?" Cartier asked as we moved to an isolated corner of the room.

"Man, this is some fuck shit. De'Asia sent out a message to someone saying she was thinking about going to the police about what La'Mea did. She never exactly said what it was, so I think that's a good thing." I tried to bring them up to speed.

"Man, that hoe. This is why I don't feel bad at all," Cartier confessed.

"You're sick, this shit is all your fucking fault!" Jakirra said, pushing Cartier. "My best friend is sitting in this nasty ass place pregnant!"

"This isn't the time nor is it the place," Ced stepped in. "Jakirra go home, I will call you when she's out."

"Shit we shoulda took care of that bitch that night with Ant, then this wouldn't even be a problem," Cartier kept going.

"That's enough," I said, pushing Cartier to back off.

We watched Jakirra collect her things and storm out. She was right, Cartier was fucked up for the shit he said, but I think we all felt like that right now. We just weren't the type to say it. We all sat down and just waited.

***

I watched so many people come in and out the double doors, I was beginning to lose count. Detective Jones sat behind his cubicle typing something on his old fashion computer. He looked up at us occasionally just to see if we were still there. We didn't move nor did we budge.

"Are ya'll waiting to see someone," a young, thick female asked, wearing a long black fitted dress with a peach blazer that matched her shoes perfectly.

"Actually, we are waiting to find out what's going on with my brother's girl. She was arrested on some bullshit." Ced stood next to the cop. "You work in this department?"

"I'm Captain Khloe Moore, and who's girlfriend?" she introduced herself.

"Mine," I stood up next to Ced. "La'Mea Black."

"Well gentlemen, she will be going to arraignment tomorrow morning, and as you know she will get a bond, and if you have the money she can be bailed out. You're wasting your time sitting down here, she's not going anywhere tonight." Khloe smiled.
I knew she was telling the truth; it was really nothing we could do. My brothers and I thanked her for the information, and we headed home.

***

I had needed a drink, so I didn't go straight home, I stopped in one of my favorite bars. Who wanted to go home alone anyway. I knew it was a chance of bumping into Monea but at that moment that didn't matter to me.

"Are you drinking alone?" Monea asked tapping my shoulder.

"Looks that way to me."

"You look like you need me to make your day better, you missed me?"

"Kinda, it really depends on how you plan on making my day better."

I took another sip of my drink. I knew what Monea had in mind and I wasn't even in the position to decline the good time I knew she was guaranteeing. I followed her out the door, we both jumped in my truck and headed to my house.

***

When we pulled up, Monea's eyes was huge. She never been to my real house that I shared with La'Mea, only down at the spot. This wasn't normal for me, between everything going on and the liquor now in my system, I wasn't really thinking. I knew La'Mea would kill me if she found out that I brought another female to our home, and I was planning to fuck her. We sat outside for a moment, a part of me wanted to say I pulled up at my nigga's house and I changed my mind, and took her to a hotel. That's what I should have done, I knew that was the more logical thing to do.

"Are we just gon' sit here or are we going to go inside, and let me put this pussy on you?" Monea asked rubbing the head of my dick, that was now standing up.

It was like the battle of right and wrong, and I knew everything about the shit I was about to do was wrong. I didn't say anything, I just motioned for her to get out and we headed inside.

***

She walked through the house completely amazed. Smiling ear to ear, she was like a kid in the candy store. She looked at the huge jacuzzi next to the patio.

"Why haven't you brought me here before?" she immediately asked looking at the décor.

"Shit I don't know, it just wasn't the right time," I said, closing off the second room off that had a lot of the babies new stuff inside.

"Well can I get a tour King Carter?" she said, slowly undressing.

"I think your tour can wait; I need you to show me those things you were talking about earlier."

Monea didn't argue, she dropped to her knees, as I slid off my grey Nike jogging pants. She started sucking and slurping on my dick. It was like everything that once was going wrong was just a memory. As much as I wasn't trying to think about La'Mea, I had to admit, when she sucked my dick she tried everything in her power to swallow my shit. Monea was cool but she wasn't her. I knew these thoughts were nothing good. It caused my dick to instantly go soft. Monea stopped and looked at me strange.

"Did I do something wrong?"

"Nah, come on, let me just hit that shit from the back really quick," I said pushing her on the couch. She did as she was told. I started fucking her from behind, forcing the thoughts of La'Mea to the back of my mind; I just wanted to get my nut off and go to sleep.

***

I didn't remember falling asleep at all, let alone leaving Monea up to give herself a tour of the house without me. I immediately jumped up and noticed she was nowhere in sight. I started to call her name but then I wouldn't know exactly what she had gotten into while I was sleep. I looked at my phone it was 6:30 a.m. I had missed three jail calls, two calls from Ced, and four calls from Jakirra. I didn't even want to look at the text messages and listen to the voicemails. I knew Monea couldn't be anywhere but upstairs considering the footsteps over my head. I knew this shit was a bad idea. I knew this shit was going to hit me in the ass later.

When I got to the top of the stairs Monea was trying to quietly close our bedroom door, I shook my head in disappointment,

"Are you looking for something?" I asked, making her jump.

"Carter," she stepped back towards the bedroom door. "I didn't know you stayed here with someone?"

"I don't see why that's your business," I said now walking towards her. "I see you decided to tour the house on your own."

"You fell asleep on me," she tried to explain.

"So again, you decided to give yourself a tour, so did you like what you see?"

"Carter who lives here with you?" she asked again.

"I don't think that's your business but let me ask you this, how long was you fucking that nigga Ant?"

Monea couldn't believe her ears, she wasn't expecting me to bring up or mention anything about Ant. I had been holding off because it just ain't been the time nor place for it, but right now was perfect. She wanted an answer and so did I.

"Ant who? I don't think I know him; I've only been fucking you?" she lied. "Now who do you live here with?"

"Imagine that, you don't know who I'm talking about. Is that your final answer because I just wanna know before I tell you the things I know."

Monea stood there for a moment, I knew she was trying to figure out how I knew about her and Ant. She wanted to ask, but she knew that wasn't the brightest thing to let come out her mouth and she really didn't want to tell me yes that was her final answer. It was like she was stuck.

"So is the girl calling you from jail your roommate?" she flipped the script.

I felt like she snatched my soul right out my chest. Did she answer the jail call?

"What girl from jail?"

"She called while you were sleep, it kept ringing, so I answered it. She sounded real upset to know you brought another girl to her home, and fucked her," she laughed. "See I don't know too much about Ant, but I do know that wifey ain't too happy with you right now."

I wanted to rip her head off. I didn't have time to play with Monea. She did the shit I hated the most. I couldn't even argue nor fight with her.

"GET OUT!" I said firmly. "Get the fuck out my shit now."

I knew she wasn't expecting that. She knew me so well that she knew that I was going to fight and fuck her.

"How am I supposed to get home? Carter you can't be serious?" she yelled, following me back downstairs. I grabbed my phone and first looked through my text messages

Jakirra: You can't be serious. I know you dont have that hoe Monea over at that house. Carter call me know. La'Mea is flipping. And how could you allow her to answer your phone.
Jakirra: Carter please call me, these bitches was just on the phone arguing, please just say you're really at the hotel and this bitch is lying
Ced: Brah,, call me, La'Mea just called me crying. She said something about Monea. Shit I could barely understand
Jakirra: Carter call me back, La'Mea is talking crazy about the baby, and not being able to take this. Please Carter call me back.
Ced: La'Mea said she's going to harm herself man, what the fuck is going on. Are you with Monea? Did you let her get your phone? Brah, you trippin' call me back! ASAP

I continued to read all the messages. I completely tuned Monea out. I dialed Ced first.

"Brah, what's going on?" he asked, sounding like he just woke up.

"Man, shit went left, I don't even know how I fell asleep and allowed this fuck shit to happen!" I begin to pace the floor. "No ifs, ands, or buts I gotta get her out, she not going to make it."

"You know her and Monea had it out. She answered every jail call that came in, she told that girl how she fucked you good in her home. La'Mea is going to kill you and that bitch. Her and Jakirra was on my phone all night. If those phones didn't automatically cut off at night they would probably still be on the phone."

"Man, I was drunk, I don't even remember fucking falling asleep. I just need to take this bitch home and head downtown."

I didn't waste more time; I didn't even want to know if Monea was really fucking with the nigga Ant. At this point it really didn't matter. I knew they said shit would get worse before it got better, shit this was ugly. I didn't even need to tell Monea once I dropped her off, we were done, and she knew it.

La'Mea

I was so angry I could strangle someone at that moment. I had been calling Carter all night, the COs were kind of nice so I got out more than I should have. I told myself if he didn't answer this time I would kill him in his sleep once I was home. I knew I was lying, I just needed him to tell me everything was going to be okay. I dialed Carter again and this time the call connected.

"Bae what were you doing? Why weren't you answering my calls?" I was annoyed.

"Sorry, baby. This ain't bae, this Monea. So, how's jail treating you?" she laughed. "Bae is passed out. I put him to sleep."

Just the sound of her voice almost made me lose it. This bitch was definitely doing some kind of drugs playing with me.

"Bitch, put Carter on the phone! Stop fucking playing with me with yo dirty ass!" I yelled through the phone.

"Bitch didn't I just tell you he was sleep. I fucked him really good in this big ass house of his, now you can call tomorrow maybe you can talk to him then."

I just knew this bitch was smoking that shit they was selling. Did she just say she fucked him really good in his big ass house? I knew that nigga wasn't this fucked up to take this dirty, scheming ass bitch to the house we called home.

"Look hoe," I started before she cut me off.

"Look bitch, don't be upset wit me, now I told you to call back. I mean I was trying to be generous because I didn't want you to waste your fifteen minutes, but baby listen, I don't have time to argue with you hoe. Now you can call OUR nigga back tomorrow," she said before hanging up.

I was hot I called back multiple times just to argue with

that bitch. I couldn't believe this nigga. I thought Jeez was a dog ass nigga. This nigga fucked the same bitch that was going to help set him up. I mean how dumb could he possibly be. I was having a break down. I knew the CO would be coming back for me soon, I called Jakirra just to see. I hadn't seen her since we walked into the justice center together.

"Best, are you okay?" she asked soon as the recording ended.

"No!" I sobbed. "I'm pregnant and in jail. And to top it off my nigga is at my house fucking another bitch."

"Stop lying, La'Mea. No he's not. Those are the hormones talking," she shot back. "Carter loves you, they stayed downtown for hours trying to see about you."

"I swear Monea, just answered his phone," I continued to sob hysterically. "She's at my house right now."

Jakirra grew quiet, I knew she was texting or telling Ced what I said.

"Call Ced and tell him what you told me. I'm about to try to call Carter. If you can, call me back okay, best. Call him now," she instructed me.

"I can't, best. Call him on three way please," I tried to pull myself together. "I don't even remember his number."

Jakirra didn't argue, she merged the calls and put her phone on mute.

"Ced, are you close to my house."

"Huh?" Ced was confused once he answered. "Jakirra?"

"No, it's La'Mea, she called on three-way, Carter is fucking Monea at my house. I can't think, I just wanna die right now. I can't do this Ced."

It was an awkward moment of silence. I knew he didn't know, and he couldn't even tell me that I didn't know what I was talking about. He knew I didn't come out the clear blue sky with these accusations, he knew I knew for sure.

"La'Mea, I don't know what you're talking about. Let me call my brother, calm down, it's not good for the baby you talking like that."

"No, what's not good for the baby is that I'm locked up here and the person I love is fucking another bitch in our house. That's what's not good for the baby!" I shouted through the phone.

I knew it wasn't Ced's fault and it wasn't nothing he could really do or say to make me feel better, it just felt good to yell and cry to someone. I felt alone and empty. Everything that I loved at this moment was on the line. I was the one in jail and it wasn't even for what I did. I never touched De'Asia, I would never touch De'Asia. Maybe this was my karma. Maybe this was God's way of punishing me for killing Ant, but then again God knew that it was an accident. I never meant to hurt Ant. I never noticed the phones cut off. I was still standing there just crying. I wanted all this to be a bad dream, but I knew it wasn't. I was taught behind every action there's a reaction and this was it. The CO walked me back to my cell, I knew I wasn't getting no sleep tonight. I laid on the hard cot alone, I couldn't even get comfortable, the tears fell from my eyes, he left me here while he was fucking off with other bitches.

***

"BLACK," the CO called my name.

I jumped up quickly, I really didn't remember falling sleep. I knew I hadn't been sleep long because I could still here the two next door to me making moaning sounds.

"Come on girl you have arraignment," she informed me. "Maybe somebody will be here waiting to bail you out."

I didn't even want to get my hopes up. I knew that Carter was probably still laid up, I didn't even bother getting on the phone. I was so hungry; they barely gave you anything. I couldn't even keep none of that shit down. My baby wasn't used to this soggy, half seasoned, half cooked shit. Just the smell of it made me nauseous.

I sat in the bullpen waiting for my turn in court, when they called my name it was like a breath of fresh air. I listen to the prosecutor tell the judge how I was withholding information that could possibly lead to the arrest on her case, all the fussing she did, my bond was only set at 5000 dollars, which was a blessing. I turned to see if I saw the boys in the back, but I saw no one. I didn't want to spend any extra time then I had to. Soon as I reached the bullpen, I called Carter. I really didn't want to talk to him but at that point I didn't have too many options, and that was only because I couldn't remember nobody's number except his and Jakirra's.

"Where are you?" I said, dryly once the call was connected.

"I'm picking up Jakirra in a minute and den we're on our way downtown to pay your bond. Are you okay?"

I hung up. It was nothing that I wanted to talk to him about. I knew he was going to feel a certain kind of way about that but hey I felt a certain kind of way. I didn't want to hear that they were on their way, they should have been here. If he wasn't laid up fucking all night he would have been here. I didn't want to hear excuses. I sat back on the cot and just waited what other choice did I have.

Carter

Man, a nigga was stressed out, I still didn't have a plug and my bitch was now in jail over this dumb ass shit. I felt like I couldn't catch a break, I needed that time with Monea, but she fucked it up being stupid. This was the shit that aggravated me and this is the type of shit that gets muthafuckas cut off. Monea didn't say shit the whole ride home. I think I might have smacked her ass out the car and made her ass walk if she did. Once we pulled up to her house she turned and looked at me.

"So, do you love her?"

"What type of question is that, Monea?"

"I mean ya'll living together. She's the reason you've been so distant with me. Like I just wanna know because I honestly thought we had something good?" she sighed.

"Tah," I chuckled.

"What the fuck is that about?"

"I mean honestly how did you think we had something good when you was fuckin' this nigga Ant behind my back? Huh?"

She was stuck; her facial expression was everything. I never told La'Mea she was right about me meeting Monea at the hotel. Shit I never even told Monea why I didn't show, but then again she never bitched about it either, and that's where I got the red flag, Monea not bitching ain't Monea.

"Oh, you didn't think I knew, huh? You didn't think I knew you was gon' set me up for that fuck nigga. Bitch." Before I could say another word, I had already had my hands around the back of her neck. "Bitch, I fucked with you, I tried to show you some different shit and you tried to fuck a nigga over."

"Carter please it wasn't like that?"

I cut her off.

"Bitch, you was sucking this nigga's dick and helping him plot against me. Bitch!" I smacked her into the window. "Hoes like you get killed like that!"

"Carter, please listen to me!" she begged.

"Nah bitch, den you over playin' yo part answering my phone and shit creeping through my shit. Bitch this ain't that." I didn't give her a chance to say shit else. "I'm cool on you. I'm just not into this shit anymore."

As soon as I released my grip on her neck, she hopped out and slammed my door. I didn't even roll the window to hear what the fuck she had to say. I needed to get downtown, I knew La'Mea already went to court and was just waiting on me. She was going to kill me for sure.

***

I thought the quickest way was the highway. I didn't even realize I was doing 85 mph until I saw those red and blue state highway patrol lights behind me.

"FUCK!" I shook my head and pulled over.

The two officers stepped out the car and approached my whip with hands on their guns, ready. It was like they were more scared to do their job now since they had been targeted.

"Is there a problem officer?"

"Yes, this is a construction zone, 50 mph. You were doing 85. License and registration please."

I knew I didn't have any worries; I got my shit cleared up weeks back, this was the unnecessary shit I didn't have time for though. I handed him my shit and rolled my window back up. I just wanted my ticket and to be on my way. La'Mea was most definitely having a whole fit, and she hadn't called either. The officers took their time issuing me the punk ass ticket. I pulled off, I was only ten minutes away if I still did at least 70, but shit knowing these thirsty bitches they would trail me for a while.

***

When I walked in to post La'Mea's bail, something didn't sit right with me. I kept feeling like I was seeing Rio, but I knew that wasn't possible because I killed that nigga. It was no saving his life. I sat in the corner and scrolled through my social media just to kill time. I never noticed the nigga that favored Rio was now standing in front of me.

"Carter!" he chuckled.

I looked up because of the mention of my name. These pigs weren't no friend of mine, they fuck was he calling my name like that for.

"Did you think it wouldn't be no repercussion to you killing my brother," he leaned in and whispered.

I looked at him in disbelief, it couldn't be, he couldn't work for the police, this shit was a joke.

"Aye brah, I think you got the wrong dude. I have no idea what the fuck you talking about," I replied defensively.

"Oh, but you do, Carter. But it's okay, that dear pregnant girlfriend of yours though, well let's just say paperwork goes missing every day." He laughed as he walked away.

I jumped up and went back to the information desk.

"How long before my girlfriend is released?"

"I'm sorry, but I can't seem to find her in the system, it's no record of her being picked up or even going to court. I was trying to do some research before I returned your money, but I don't have a La'Mea Black in the system." The receptionist slid the money back under the glass.

"Man, ya'll got me fucked up. My pregnant girlfriend is down here. She wasn't released. She called me from jail!" I looked around for Rio's people.

I spotted that nigga in the corner with the same detective that arrested La'Mea. I watched them laugh as I stood at the window.

"Is there someone else I can talk to, that bitch ass cop right there arrested her. She's down here, they set her bond, man."

"I apologize, maybe she's at another jail," she said, closing down her window. "If you get some more information please do come back, I will be more than happy to help."

I was pissed off, I couldn't believe this shit, La'Mea was a sitting duck down in this bitch. I reached for my phone just as it started to ring, it was Cartier.

"Brah, what's up, I was just about to call you."

"Brah, they hit Ced man. I'm on my way to the hospital. What the fuck is going on? These niggas know not to try us."

My heart stopped. My fucking brother, my pregnant girl, this shit was getting really ugly, it was like the beginning to the end. Karma.

Made in the USA
Monee, IL
10 November 2020

47147343R00066